CONSTABLE
IN THE
WILDERNESS

A perfect feel-good read from one of
Britain's best-loved authors

NICHOLAS RHEA

Constable Nick Mystery Book 28

JOFFE
BOOKS

Revised edition 2021
Joffe Books, London
www.joffebooks.com

First published in Great Britain in 2003
by Robert Hale Limited

ISBN: 978-1-78931-936-1

CHAPTER 1

Mary answered the jangling telephone because I was outside.
I was knee deep in fresh deep snow and struggling against
bitter gale-force winds as I tried in vain to excavate a path
through huge drifts. Powdery waves of snow smothered the
drive of our exposed hilltop police house, effectively blocking
the entrance to the garage, and also smothering the footpaths
which led to our front door and my office. As I worked,
the ever-present wind made my task impossible. As fast as
I cleared a patch, the blasts of wind blew the snow back in
again and I began to wonder if I'd ever clear a route from the
house. I began to feel I was fighting a losing battle.

The overnight fall, not entirely unexpected, had been
accompanied by the powerful north wind which had soon
whipped the new snow into formidable drifts along the ridge
of the hill upon which my home stood. It was like living on
the edge of a wilderness—all I could see beyond my home was
a pure white landscape but even without the wind the heavy
snowfall would have blocked roads, cut off remote farms,
forced down powerlines and effectively brought country life
to a halt, particularly in the more exposed parts of the moors.
As it was, the wind had come with a vengeance to exacerbate
the problem. I'd learned there were drifts twelve-feet high in

1

places with sheep buried, lorries and their drivers marooned on moorland roads, and people in remote communities cut off from civilization as the network of narrow roads had become impassable. And the blizzard was still raging.

My colleagues at Ashfordly were coping as best they could and Alf Ventress had telephoned to provide an update of the situation, adding, 'Stay put, Nick, you're more use to us at the end of a telephone than marooned in a snowdrift somewhere on the moors. There's not much we can do until the snowploughs and gritters have been, and I'm told even they are having trouble getting through in some places.'

I told him I would spend time trying to dig myself out. Meanwhile the County Council's Highways Department was responding with gritters, snowploughs and huge machines designed to literally blow the snow from the roads and into the neighbouring fields or on to the wasteland of the moors. RAF helicopters were standing by to drop food and bedding to marooned sheep and cattle and, if necessary, transport any trapped humans or birth-giving mothers to safety.

As I well knew, the emergency services and council highways personnel could not be everywhere at once and certain places demanded priority treatment such as routes to hospitals, access for the emergency services and routes to shops which could provide food and clothing. Such essentials might be required for an emergency situation if people had to be evacuated to safety in village halls or community centres; consequently it was vital that these commodities were accessible.

With generations of experience to call upon, the people of the North York Moors were accustomed to periodic heavy snowfalls which invariably resulted in severe drifting and blocked roads on the higher ground. During the late autumn months they would prepare for a prolonged period of isolation by accumulating stocks of food, fuel like wood and coal, and good thick warm clothing.

Some of these people could exist for three months without any form of human contact if necessary—and sometimes it was necessary with drifts, gales and falling snow dominating December, January and February. Farmers had to consider livestock which might have to be cared for during an extended period—sufficient bedding and food had to be stockpiled for them. If the general public felt that, with the lighter nights of February, winter was coming to an end, the wise old farmers knew otherwise; for them, Candlemas Day (2 February) was merely the halfway stage of winter. They always said a good moorland farmer should have half the animals' fodder and half their bedding left in stock at Candlemas because there was still a lot of bad weather ahead.

Almost certainly, if there was a heavy snowfall, the electricity supplies would be cut off, consequently oil lamps, Calor gas cookers generators and other means of providing a reserve supply of power and heat were vital for survival in the wilder parts of the moors. The very isolated moorland farms became like castles under siege. Milking could be a problem for dairy farms too, particularly those who relied on electricity, while disposal of the fresh milk was another huge worry. Several moorland farmers possessed their own snowploughs which they attached to a tractor to clear the tracks leading to their premises and perhaps those of their neighbours—this, coupled with the clearing of other routes, usually meant the milk did leave the premises, but not without difficulty. With the onset of winter, therefore, local shops did a massive trade in paraffin, tinned food, cured ham, sacks of potatoes and other durable foodstuffs as the locals made their emergency preparations.

Those living on the higher and more remote parts of the moors were very skilled at survival in atrocious conditions and many had a siege-like mentality which sprang into action at the first sign of a frost or snowflake. In general terms, therefore, the people of the moors were the ones for whom the authorities need show the least concern; they were extremely capable of looking after themselves.

The real problems were often generated at a lower altitude. A mere inch of snow in the city centre or suburbs of

York could cause havoc and bring the city to a standstill amid stories of ferocious weather. In general, people living on the lower ground and in seaside towns, as well as those living in the south of England (i.e. that part to the south of York) had no concept of conditions on the moors during, say, a raging blizzard, or even a moderately heavy snowfall. Certainly they had no idea how to cope with an unexpectedly and truly heavy fall of snow.

In my case that morning in late January, I felt rather like one of those farmers coping somewhere in a limitless white wilderness, but, of course, my problems were as nothing compared with any of those high moorland dwellers. Certainly, we'd had something akin to a blizzard in the early hours; it was not quite of North Pole severity but enough to cause disruption to domestic life in and around my home. More to the point, it was still snowing and still blowing as my puny efforts revealed. My drive was under more than two feet of snow 'reg'lar away' as the locals termed it. It was still blowing into drifts against the doors and north-facing walls of the house; in front of the garage those drifts rose the height of the doors, seven feet or so, and they spread about five feet back from the doors into the drive.

It was a massively thick wall of snow even though the hedge along the side of the road beyond the lawn had sheltered the house from the worst of the onslaught. To forge a route from the garage would require a huge effort over some considerable time. I had to dig a route through the mass and get rid of it all too, as the wind would undoubtedly continue to frustrate most of my attempts. Wherever I dumped the shovelfuls of snow, the wind would blow them apart and return everything to its former place. I began to ponder the wisdom of working against such odds.

Even if I did manage to dig a route from the garage, I could not leave the house by motor vehicle because the road outside was well and truly blocked. It was covered in huge wave-like drifts stretching from hedge to hedge and so, if I was to go anywhere by motor vehicle, I would have to wait until that road, and the others to which it was linked, were ploughed. The road just outside my house ran along the summit of a rigg, the local name for an elevated ridge of land, and because it passed between two high hedges it was inevitably blocked during a heavy snowfall when wind was a factor.

As I sweated and worked to clear my drive, there was no sign of a plough—this stretch of road was of low priority in such matters—but I had to make my effort because in time the road would be cleared sufficiently for traffic to use it. I knew I had to be prepared for that moment because I might be called out to help someone in a worse situation. As things were, however, I was now one of those people whom the press would describe as living on higher ground and cut off by Arctic-like blizzard conditions.

As a policeman, however, I was supposed to be on duty and patrolling my patch around Aidensfield, but I considered that my immediate priority was to clear all the entrances to my house. Ashfordly police office staff knew where I was and were aware of the situation. Clad in my most protective clothing over my uniform, I continued with my unproductive efforts to clear the snow and in spite of the wind, I began to feel I was making some slight progress. As I did my utmost to throw spadefuls over the garden hedge into an adjoining field or heave it on to the lawn, the kitchen window opened and Mary called as a blast of wind sent a cloud of snow towards her. 'It's the superintendent, he's on the phone. He wants a word.'

'Now?' I shouted against the fierce gust.

'Yes, now,' she said, slamming the window to prevent snow from filling the kitchen.

I trudged towards my office entrance with my head down against the blast, at times up to my thighs in drifts, and I parked my shovel against the outer wall of the house then leapt inside, opening and shutting the door with the maximum possible speed to prevent the snow blowing in. Some did accompany me indoors and a few massive lumps also fell from my clothing as I made for the office. Doing my best to avoid dropping any more snow, especially on to the polished floor, but failing miserably, I saw the phone lying on my desk.

'PC Rhea, Aidensfield,' I panted into it.

'It's the superintendent, Rhea,' said the voice at the other end. 'Glad I caught you before you go out on patrol. I want a word with you. Now, as I am about to drive to head-quarters to a conference with the chief constable, I thought I would call on you *en route*, say, in three quarters of an hour? Before your office period is over.'

Whenever we performed a tour of duty directly from our police houses, we were allowed the first hour in the office attached to the house. This meant we could complete any outstanding paperwork and it also enabled us to be contacted if required, either by members of the public or our own staff. Although I had begun my digging operations long before my tour of duty was supposed to start, I was now at the start of my official hour of office duty. It was just nine o'clock.

'Sir,' I was still panting from my efforts. 'Sir, there's been a heavy fall of snow here, I'm having to dig myself out and the road past my house is blocked, the plough hasn't been through yet. I understand heavy falls and severe drifting are widespread around the moors.'

'I have received reports from most of the sub-division, Rhea, but if I understand things correctly, the problems are restricted to the very high ground, the upper regions of the moorland. There's no snow here, and I'm less than thirty minutes' drive from you. You shouldn't let a bit of snow hinder your duties, Rhea, and you shouldn't exaggerate the situation, not to an old hand like me. I've faced more snow-bound roads and drifts than you've had hot dinners, so, as I said, I'll be with you in forty-five minutes.'

'But sir,' I began to plead with him, 'sir, I'm not exaggerating, we've got a gale-force wind up here and there's more than two feet of level snow and some dreadful drifts on the higher roads. It's still snowing too, a real blizzard.'

'As I have just pointed out, Rhea, we have nothing down here at all. It's a lovely day, ideal for a drive across the moors to Police Headquarters. Quarter to ten, then,' and he put down his telephone.

It was a fact that snowstorms on our moors could be very isolated, with heavy falls in some areas and nothing a few miles away. During the course of any winter, one could view the moorland heights from a distance and see them capped with snow while the lower ground basked in sunshine. It was rather like looking at the snow-capped Alps from afar; the Pennines, high above the Yorkshire Dales, could produce a similar effect—beautiful white peaks overlooking the sunshine which bathed the lower ground. It seemed that today was one of those occasions on our moors. At times, the difference between the weather on the heights of the moors and the bottom of the Dales could be amazing. Furthermore, wind-driven storms could move rapidly across the heights, obliterating one area before moving to another a few minutes later and I suspected the present conditions were of that kind. We were having a real blizzard of a fast-moving storm while, according to my boss less than twenty miles away, there was none. With that in mind, I stared at the handset and was in two minds about my next course of action. I could forget all about shovelling snow and let my superintendent see how far he got—he'd never reach my house this morning unless the road outside was ploughed very soon.

However, my sense of responsibility overcame such reactionary thoughts and I decided I should continue with my digging so that my paths and drive were clear. That had to be done for my family's convenience and if my boss did arrive, it would show him that I had not been idle. Deciding that a cup of hot coffee might be a good idea before resuming my efforts, Mary managed to produce one in a very short time as the children played in the lounge and watched the storm outside, wondering when they could go sledging down the neighbouring field. Standing dripping in my office as I enjoyed the drink, I told Mary I was going to resume my onslaught upon the drifts. Making sure I was well wrapped from head to toe, that my wellington boot tops were covered with my police issue leggings to prevent snow falling inside, and that my neck was encased in a thick scarf in such a way that no snow could be blown down my body by even the fiercest wind, I sallied forth once more.

I opened the door and the wind whipped it from my grasp before thrusting in a whole cloud of snow as I lurched outside and managed to slam it shut. Then I couldn't find my shovel. The wind had blown it over and it had fallen into the soft new snow; even during the short time I had been absent, it had been covered and was nowhere in sight. I tried wading through the soft snow with my feet flailing alternatively to left and right, hoping a foot might make contact with the shovel and after some five or six minutes, I found it. Reinforced by my coffee, my shovel and the fact the superintendent was intending to visit me, I resumed my efforts.

Then quite suddenly, after I'd been labouring for a further half-hour or so, the wind dropped and it stopped snowing. I stood in some amazement as the storm swept away towards the east. I could see its tail-end, a thick mass of black clouds being swept along and depositing tons of snow on the landscape spread below me. But now I was standing in fair, if a little dull, weather, and there was no wind to whip the snow into my recently cleared areas. From my privileged viewpoint on the hilltop site, I could look down upon a landscape of pure white with roofs and trees covered, the only dark areas being the lee side of the hedges, pine forests and the sheltered sides of churches and other buildings. For some considerable time, I stood in the silence to absorb the spectacular scene. It was like some gigantic white quilt and I knew it smothered roads, paths, houses, fields and even entire villages, but soon the ploughs would arrive, people would begin to move; roads would be cleared to make dark tracks through the whiteness, vehicles would resume their journeys, the snow would melt in places too, to fill the rivers, becks and ditches.

With no more snow falling and a lack of wind, I reckoned life would be almost back to normal around twelve noon. It was amazing how soon normality returned in such situations and so I bent to my task with renewed vigour. I was now fortified by the knowledge that I was making an impact on the accumulated snow and must admit I forgot the passage of time. As I worked, the children emerged in their allegedly snow-proof clothing; they wanted to go sledging down a neighbouring field but I felt the snow was far too deep and, at this stage, far too soft to cope with toboggans.

Apart from anything else, their sledges were in the garage and, at this stage, quite beyond my reach, and so at my suggestion, they settled for building a large snowman on the lawn, making use of the huge pile of snow I had deposited there. I told them I might even find an old police helmet for him to wear and felt sure I could locate a piece of wood to act as his truncheon. He would become a guardian policeman, a figure of authority outside our house.

The abrupt change in the weather meant I began to make speedier headway with clearing the drive before tackling the monster drift in front of the garage doors. As I worked, a snowplough came past, its noise being a most welcome sound as it thrust the virgin snow to the sides of the road to make at least one carriageway passable. Things were improving by the minute, but then there was a problem with the snowman.

Elizabeth, my eldest child, shouted, 'Dad, he won't stand up. We can't get him to stand up and we want him to have a head and arms.'

When I looked across at their efforts, most of it achieved by hand albeit with a little help from a coal shovel, I realized they'd given the snowman a base which was far too narrow. They were trying to make him stand tall and erect by making him a thin character, whereas they really needed a very broad base which could become narrower towards the top. I explained that the broader his bottom, the taller he could stand, even with a little help from a stool to reach his higher regions. I saw this creation needed some timely help and so I abandoned my own task temporarily and began to explain this highly scientific construction technique to the children.

My teaching was aided by shovelfuls of snow which I packed around the base, smacking the growing pile with the back of the shovel to make it as firm as possible while continuing my demonstration of the skills of snowman construction. Soon, we were doing very well indeed. The children understood what was required and we all packed more snow around the base and hammered it hard with the back of my shovel, producing a huge and highly impressive snowman right on my lawn, almost in front of my office door. I told them I had an old disused helmet upstairs in my wardrobe, wondering if all they would do would be to throw snowballs at it to knock it off. After a time, I felt very proud of this sculpted giant.

'It's the superintendent!' shouted Elizabeth, as we began to fashion the head.

'It's more like Claude Jeremiah Greengrass!' I laughed.

'No, it's the superintendent, Dad, he's covered in snow and he looks just like this—'

'It is the superintendent!' bellowed a voice behind me and I whirled around to find my boss standing at the garden gate. There was no sign of a car. He was dressed in his ordinary civilian suit with low shoes on his feet and a useless raincoat as a pathetic form of protection against the elements. Even though the blizzard had stopped, he was smothered from head to toe and looked like something the dog had dragged in from beneath a snowdrift.

'Oh, sir.' I did not know what to say. 'Er, hello, sir . . .'

'Is this what you call duty, Rhea? Building a snowman?'

'Er, no, sir, I was clearing the drive, trying to get to my garage . . .'

'It didn't look like that to me, Rhea! I would say you were building a snowman when you should have been patrolling your beat! If you couldn't get your van out, you could always use your feet, you know, the road has been ploughed.'

'Yes, sir, but it was just a few minutes ago.' I knew that, like the snowman, I didn't have a leg to stand on and instead of trying to justify my actions, I opted for a show of concern.

'You'd better come in, sir, you look soaked and cold. Where's your car?'

'It's in a snowdrift somewhere down the road,' and he waved his arms as if to indicate the general direction. 'I must have walked miles; you never told me it was as bad as this, Rhea.'

'I tried, sir, but you said—'

'Never mind what I said!' He did not sound at all happy. 'Just get me inside, let me use your telephone and . . .'

'I think a cup of coffee is a good idea, sir, and we can perhaps dry some of your clothes while you're here.' And so I trudged through the snow, still two-feet deep where it was level and several feet high where there were drifts against the house. Mary was in the kitchen and had witnessed this little drama outside the window. She'd had the wisdom to put on the kettle straight away. A cup of tea or coffee could work wonders on such occasions. Another bonus was that the coke boiler in the kitchen which served as our heating, was throwing out a good deal of warmth and I felt he could at least dry some of his clothes, even if it meant standing close to it. The coal fire was also burning in the lounge where the children had been playing.

As I escorted my boss through the deep snow, his soaking shoes getting filled with even more and his trouser bottoms even more soaked, Mary opened the front door and met us in the porch.

'Good heavens.' She looked at him. 'You look soaked to the skin, Mr Proctor, come in. Take him into the lounge, Nick; I'll take your coat, sir.'

We removed our outer clothes as best we could in the confines of the entrance hall; beneath my layers of waterproofs and weatherproofs, I was quite dry and warm, but Superintendent Proctor was soaking from the knees downwards. His mackintosh, designed more for deterring showers in an urban environment, had repelled most of the weather and so his suit jacket and trousers down to his knees were dry; the neck of his shirt was wet, however, and his hair was hanging down his face like rats' tails, while his feet, shoes, socks and gloves were soaking and cold.

Mary was wonderful. With her common sense, feminine charm and hours of practice dealing with children in this kind of situation, she persuaded my boss to remove his socks and shoes, and to put on my slippers while his socks dried near the fire. His gloves and shoes might dry a little too, while his trousers could dry around his legs, if he stood close enough to the hearth. Quite suddenly, I found myself in a very domestic situation with my sorry-looking boss who appeared anything but officious or official as he stood there with steam rising from his trouser bottoms, no socks on and my slippers on his feet. His mackintosh was on a coat hanger above the coke boiler in the kitchen, and my outer clothes were relegated to the downstairs toilet until somewhere else could be found for them.

He hadn't reminded me about wanting to use the telephone, and so, when Mary produced coffee for us and he sat in a chair, still with his legs near the blazing fire, I asked, 'Sir, your car. Obviously, you walked here from somewhere. It will need to be recovered.'

'I was going to ring Divisional Headquarters and get them to send a breakdown truck. There's no damage, it's just stuck in a drift and I think the front wheels are in a ditch.'

'We might get a local farmer and his tractor to pull you out. Is it far away?'

From what he told me, it seemed he had been heading towards Aidensfield, climbing the long road which rose several hundred feet from the bottom of the dale to run along the top of the rigg, when he'd been literally overwhelmed by the sudden blizzard of thick wind-driven snow. He said it was a whiteout; he could not see ahead and suddenly found himself driving into deep snowdrifts.

'I couldn't see a thing, Rhea; now I know what a whiteout is really like. So I decided to pull into the side of the road until I could see, or until the storm had passed. Sadly, it was covered in deep snow, and there was a ditch, it was hidden by the snow and I ran into it. I'm sure there's no damage to the car.'

He had been unable to extricate the vehicle on his own and so he had decided to walk to my house which he knew lay along the road, around a mile and a half ahead.

'I tried to radio Control but couldn't get a signal, so here I am, Rhea, looking like a drowned rat and feeling something of an idiot.'

'Well, there's no real problem, sir,' I tried to reassure him. 'The plough has been through and the road is partially open; the storm is heading further east and we can drag your car out in no time. I can't get into my garage yet, but there are plenty of farmers hereabouts who'll lend a hand with a tractor. And it might be wise to cancel your journey to head-quarters, even if the plough does clear the roads; they'll still be very treacherous and it could blow in again if the wind turns.'

By the time we had discussed his predicament and enjoyed two cups of coffee and some biscuits, his socks and gloves had dried, but his shoes remained wet. His trouser bottoms were drier and his mackintosh was still steaming in the kitchen.

'I have to walk back to the car anyway.' He was now smiling. 'This is not the ideal clothing for walking in these conditions but it's my own fault. So, you said you knew a farmer who might help?'

'Harry Newton at Thackerston,' I said. 'From what you've told me, I think you are somewhere close to his farm.'

'Is that better than calling out a local garage?' he asked.

'I think any garage will be inundated with emergency calls right now, sir, so I think Harry would be best for you. You won't have to join a queue for his services either.'

And so I rang Harry. He was at home and had already spotted the black official-looking Ford in the ditch at the top of one of his fields.

When I explained the situation, he readily offered to help with his tractor and even offered to come to my house to collect the superintendent to prevent him having to walk all the way back to his car. I said I would come too, in case several hands were required to retrieve the vehicle. And so it was, as my children put their finishing touches to their snowman, I jumped aboard a tractor with my superintendent joining me in his wet shoes, and together we chugged along the snowbound lane to where his car awaited; the plough had been right through and there was a reasonably clear carriageway. It was the work of a few minutes for the tractor to haul the car from the snowdrift, another few minutes for us to make sure it was facing the right way for the superintendent to return home—although I did remind him that the storm had been travelling in the same direction, the only concession being that as it blew towards the east, it was heading for lower ground. At sea level, it might be nothing but heavy rain. The superintendent thanked Harry and gave him a £1 note for his trouble, and then Harry offered to take me home. I said I would appreciate the lift.

'Oh, Rhea,' said the superintendent as an afterthought. 'I almost forgot. The reason I had to talk to you. As you might not yet have heard, Sergeant Craddock is going away on a management course, he'll be away for six months. I would like you to be acting sergeant in the Ashfordly section during his absence. Will you do that?'

'Acting sergeant, sir?'

'Yes, you're qualified, you've had a good deal of experience and it will make sure your name is before the right people when your future is considered further.'

'Well, er, yes, sir. Thank you, yes.'

'Good. Well, I will notify you officially when it is due to take effect, probably within a week or two from now. It won't be as easy as you think, you realize; it's rather like casting a child into the wilderness and leaving him to cope, no one is quite sure what is lying in wait out there. But I am sure you will cope; six months is a long time and it will be a good test of your skills. And, of course, you will receive a pay increase during your temporary promotion. Meanwhile, thank you for helping me like this, I'm sure my plight will reach other ears before too long! But right now, you'd better get back to your other snowman. And can you ring the chief constable, please, at headquarters, to explain my absence from his conference?'

'The chief constable, sir?'

'It's your first challenge as a potential sergeant, Rhea. You failed to convince me of the true state of the weather up here, let's see if you can convince him.'

'I'll do my best, sir,' I muttered, as I climbed aboard Harry's tractor.

CHAPTER 2

Problems with moorland snowfalls did not end with the clearing of the roads and footpaths because if there was a rapid thaw following even moderate deposits, some flooding was inevitable. If the thaw was gentle, however, the resultant water could be absorbed into the landscape or funnelled into existing channels and drains without any dramatic effect, other than the rivers and streams being full of what the local people called 'a fair bit o' fresh watter'. This 'fresh watter' was welcome so long as it did not overflow; a full, fast flowing river was one means of getting rid of rubbish which had accumulated over a long period. Things like broken tree branches, waste vegetation, assorted litter, the carcasses of dead animals, discarded junk and so forth were flushed out and washed downstream, usually vanishing beneath the surface for ever, or broken up by strong water before reaching the North Sea. Full and fast flowing rivers were therefore welcome; floods were not.

Large-scale flooding was rare on my patch at Aidensfield although the occasional problem did arise through blocked drains on the roads when surfaces could disappear under a few inches or even a foot or so. Another concern was the courses of small becks which had become obstructed by fallen trees, dislodged rocks or even man-made dams erected by children and parents while enjoying the countryside in summer. These minor waterways could overflow and cause problems to houses, farms, gardens and buildings along their banks. Further away, however, much of the Vale of Pickering, including towns like Malton and Norton on the banks of the River Derwent, had for centuries been subjected to regular flooding.

This persisted into modern times in spite of work by Sir George Cayley of Brompton near Scarborough. He devised a remarkable solution to the risk of flooding by the River Derwent in his construction of the Derwent Sea Cut which remains to this day. Between 1800 and 1810, a channel was cut by hand from Everley to Scalby Mills near Scarborough and a sluice allows the normal waters of the Derwent to run along their course but any excess flows over the sluice and heads into the safety of the North Sea at Scalby, some five miles away. Sir George's scheme has prevented large-scale flooding since its inception and it still remains highly effective in winter when the moors act as a huge catchment area for water released by melting snow. The moors can discharge massive amounts of water into the Derwent which, in spite of the Sea Cut, then overflows its banks to flood towns like Malton and Norton or even villages much further downriver such as Stamford Bridge. In addition, York is also prone to spectacular flooding because the Ouse accepts massive amounts from other rivers like the Ure, Swale, Aire and their tributaries; consequently, if it snows then thaws quickly in the Yorkshire Dales, the citizens of York can expect yet another severe flood or two. Water flowing from snow thawing high in the Dales in the west and from the North York Moors in the east, can therefore produce misery for people living a long way from both those areas.

However, the snow which had so inconvenienced my superintendent did not present any undue problems when it melted because it was a gentle thaw which allowed much of the water to seep into the ground, any excess being easily accommodated by the natural outlets. Indeed, this kind of slow melt is considered beneficial by landowners and gardeners. In addition to keeping the ground moist in winter when it acts as a kind of warm overblanket, it also enables water to sink gradually into the earth instead of flowing away or merely touching the surface, and while soaking into the ground, it carries into the earth various nutrients which it absorbs from the air. Many country people believe that a fall of snow which melts gradually is as good as a load of manure on the land.

If, after a thaw however, patches of snow linger in hollows on the moor or in the shelter of drystone walls and similar places shaded from the sun, then the moorfolk say, 'It'll need another fall to get rid of it.' And so it transpired that year. There were several heavy falls during January and February, none of which resulted in severe flooding but as the days lengthened in March, we suffered a very heavy and rather unseasonal fall on the higher parts of the moors. Seasoned rustics nodded their heads in sage-like wisdom and pronounced the snow had been necessary to clear away the remnants of earlier falls and although that March did not produce any other snows, that lone and very heavy fall created the usual problems. Livestock were marooned, most being still in their shippens, but sheep out on the wilds of the moor had to be hand fed because the snow was too deep for them to penetrate to the ground for food. Bales of hay were hauled on to the moors by tractor and distributed for them to enjoy. A pregnant woman was air-lifted from an isolated farm by helicopter and taken to the maternity hospital where she gave birth to twins, much to the delight of everyone. A pair of ramblers got lost, later turning up safe and sound, but cold and hungry, in a disused barn—these were all normal dramas in a fairly normal winter.

While the moors remained covered in snow, however, the sunshine was growing stronger by the day as spring approached and then, quite suddenly, we had three days of very hot sunshine. This even warmed the air high on the moors and the accumulated snow began to melt very quickly, and people in the floors of the dales below were unaware of what was happening on the moors high around them.

My short spell of temporary promotion, during which I wore two stripes on my arm to denote my elevated position, had hitherto been unremarkable. I had compiled the Ashfordly section duty roster for the weeks ahead, made sure the office was staffed efficiently, undertook some elementary supervisory tasks and checked the written reports of my colleagues before submitting them to the inspector at Eltering. Unlike a substantive sergeant in charge of his own section, I did not prosecute in court, present evidence at inquests or undertake the duties expected of a senior sergeant. After all, I was only temporarily acting in the rank, but I must admit I felt as if I'd not done anything exceptional or noteworthy, although there was some time left for nail-biting drama and high excitement before Sergeant Craddock's return.

That drama came from melting snow high on the moors. In my new role, I was expected to pay the occasional visit to my sub-divisional headquarters in Eltering, perhaps for a discussion with the inspector about some professional matter or ongoing problem, or perhaps he wanted to talk about a new initiative. He was very good at listening to new ideas.

On the other hand, he might even instruct me to undertake a supervisory role over the constables patrolling the town in the temporary absence of the local shift sergeant. It was all very interesting and a welcome change from the normal routine of my work in the quiet of rural Aidensfield. One Saturday evening during that March, therefore, I was in the police station at Eltering. It was a few minutes after nine o'clock and I was due to go off duty at ten; on the drive into Eltering about an hour earlier, I had paid supervisory visits to a couple of patrolling constables, and had also brought some paperwork to Eltering which I had deposited in the inspector's in-tray. Likewise, I had collected some files for return to Ashfordly and, having completed all my modest tasks, was about to leave the office to drive home when the phone rang. The duty constable answered it.

'Eltering Police, PC Rogers,' he said.

I waited just in case it was something requiring my attention, and then John Rogers said, 'Just a minute, sir, we have someone of authority here. I'll put him on,' and he looked across to me. 'For you, Nick.' He grinned with just a hint of mischief. 'It's a man who's insisting on speaking to someone in authority,' and he passed the handset to me.

'Acting Sergeant Rhea,' I responded, with all the authority I could muster.

'Acting Sergeant?' boomed the deep male Yorkshire voice at the other end. 'I was expecting an inspector at least, a superintendent if possible. Are you the highest ranking officer there, Mr Rhea?'

'At the moment, yes I am. Might I ask who's calling?'

'Arnold Snape from High Rigg,' he said. 'And this is important, lad, very important, so if you're all I've got to talk to I'd better get on with it, and then you'd better make sure you do summat sharpish.'

'High Rigg?' I said, and John Rogers pointed to a map on the wall behind the telephone, his finger showing me exactly where to find the address. It was several miles out of Eltering, in a remote and very wild part of the moors, a long way from any village. 'I know the area, north of Eltering. A very isolated farmstead.'

'That's me, now, young man, you'd better get things moving because I've just been down my fields and there's a beck full of fresh water down there, overflowing in places, and running like the clappers. If I know my water, and my moors, then all this lot'll have come off that snow higher up. It's on its way down to you, with more coming down Eltering Beck and much more to come later tonight and even tomorrow from all that melting snow. Not just from my beck, mark you, it'll come from all the other becks up here. There's lots of 'em. And you know what all that adds up to, Acting Sergeant Rhea?'

'Er, well, no, not really,' I had to admit.

'It means your town centre's going to be flooded with two or three foot of mucky water in about three or four hours from now. So that's why I'm ringing, so you can do summat about it.'

'Are you sure?' I must admit I wondered whether or not I should heed this warning. After all, people did ring us with all kinds of amateurish advice, and I wondered how a rise of the water level in a beck high on those moors could produce a town-centre flood several miles away in such a short time.

'Sure?' he bellowed. 'I've never been so sure in my life. So there you are, you can't say you weren't warned; it's building up fast,' and he put the phone down.

'What's he want?' asked John Rogers, when he saw the expression on my face.

'It's a man called Arnold Snape,' I said. 'He says the beck on his land is full of fresh water which is rising fast from melting snow and he thinks there'll be a flood down here tonight, in the town centre, two or three feet deep he reckons. He said we should expect it about midnight, or just after, unless we do something about it.'

'Do something about it? What can we do about that?' he cried.

'Evacuate the town centre, that's because he mentioned the town centre in particular. We can get sandbags arranged; call the emergency services to stand by; get the fire brigade to pump the water away, the council to find accommodation for the evacuees, civil defence to arrange food and blankets . . .'

'Hang on, Nick, isn't this a bit drastic? How can we believe the word of this man? Do you know him? I must admit I don't. How do we know he's reliable? How do we know he's genuine? We're going to look right Charlies if we create a lot of panic and confusion for no good reason.'

'And we're going to look even worse Charlies if Snape is right and we do nothing about it,' I countered. 'Right, first things first. Is there a contingency plan anywhere in our files?'

'What sort of contingency?' he frowned. 'We've nothing to cover this kind of situation, I can tell you that.'

'How about an operational order of any kind, something drawn up to cope with any sort of emergency situation?

There must be something in the files. Can you have a look before I decide what to do next? And meanwhile, I'm going to ring Alf Ventress, he's on duty in Ashfordly right now.'

'Alf? What does he know about this?'

'He's got a bottomless pit of a memory for things that have happened around here in the past, John, he might recall a similar event. It's worth a call.'

'Right, I'll see what's in our system. I'll try the Major Incident files.'

'There's no time to lose, John,' I reminded him. 'If this is a real threat, we'll have to get moving fast.'

To give him credit, John did take things seriously—I could judge that by the expression on his face—and I began to wonder if we sounded like the little Dutch boy who blocked a tiny hole in the dam with his finger to stop the flow of water which would bring down the entire structure to devastate the area. How could a couple of policemen prevent this kind of flood? We couldn't stand in the middle of the beck to halt the water with our big flat feet, so there must be some other way. That's why I rang Alf to test his powers of recall.

'Oh, yes, I remember 1947,' said Alf, after I had explained the situation. 'The whole town centre was awash with water coming down from High Rigg and elsewhere as the snow melted. Arnold's right, you know, you'll have to do something, Nick.'

'So why the town centre?'

'It's the culvert under the bottom of the main street, it's too narrow to take all the flood water when it comes in large quantities all at once, and it spills over into the road and town. It happened in 1947, Nick, I remember it well. It could have been prevented if they'd known about it earlier. You need sandbags along the banks in the town centre, but the trick is to divert High Rigg Beck higher up the valley.'

'Divert the beck? We haven't time to do that!' I stressed.

'Yes you have. There's an old watercourse up there, where the beck used to run, and after the 1947 experience, they put a huge bank of sandbags there to divert the flood water into that old watercourse, and it worked: 1952 that was. It saved the town on that occasion. Now if you can just repeat that 1952 procedure, Nick, your reputation will be assured. The King Canute of Eltering, so to speak. But if I was you, I'd call the inspector. Let him make all the decisions, Nick, this one's a bit out of your league, although you could start by alerting the council offices to get sandbags organized. They keep a stock you know, always ready and waiting for such occasions, and then there's the question of evacuating the town-centre properties.'

I remember thinking during those moments that there should be some kind of official advance warning system for cases of flooding because all I had to rely upon was the opinion of a man who lived high on the moors. Then I thought of my superintendent who had not appreciated my warning about the snow on the hills around my house, and in addition, I was vividly aware of the old adage, 'Better safe than sorry'.

And so, while John Rogers was hunting for some kind of pre-arranged emergency plan which would provide guidance in this kind of situation, I rang the out-of-hours number at the council offices.

'Fenton,' said a man's voice.

'Police,' I said. 'Eltering Police, Acting Sergeant Rhea. We've an emergency, we need sandbags,' and I provided an explanation of the reason, along with Alf's recommended positioning of the sandbags.

'We need more than that before we call out our teams,' he said. 'You've just got the opinion of some old chap living on the moors who's probably had a chicken coop washed away. Remember it means overtime payments and other expenses of various kinds. Then there's the question of evacuation of those town-centre properties, you chaps going round with megaphones to get the residents to leave their homes and shops, calling out the fire brigade to pump cellars out, civil defence to do their bit . . . what sort of authority can you offer before I press the panic button, Acting Sergeant Rhea?'

'Authority?' I was puzzled for a moment. I had no authority, I knew that. I was acutely aware that I was responding like this merely on the knowledge of one senior police constable with a good memory, and a man of the moors who seemed to know what he was talking about. Then I had a flash of inspiration, the sort that comes to mind only once in a while.

'We must have some kind of authority before I put our emergency plans into operation,' Fenton stressed.

'1947,' I responded. 'And then 1952.'

'Good God, yes! The snow melted suddenly on the moors and the next thing we knew the town centre was awash . . . I remember that. We need to sandbag the beck upstream, don't we? I know the place. We divert flood water into that old dried-up watercourse as we did in 1952, we put sandbags along the banks of the beck where it passes through the town, alert residents to the likelihood of being evacuated . . . right, Acting Sergeant Rhea, leave it with me. We don't want another 1947, do we?'

'We do not!' I hoped my voice sounded full of authority.

Meanwhile John Rogers had found a file which was called 'Major Incident Plan' which was the nearest thing he could link to the likely threat which faced us, and as we pored over the orders within, we realized we were doing the right things so far as the emergency services were concerned, although it made no reference to sandbagging the beck somewhere in the hills.

'I'm calling the inspector now,' I told John, 'then I'll call Control Room, they'll have their own call-out procedures.'

Inspector Harry Breckon answered the phone in his own private house.

'Breckon,' he said.

'It's Acting Sergeant Rhea, sir, speaking from Eltering,' and I explained the situation to him.

I told him what I had done and he responded with, 'I hope you've not exceeded your authority, Acting Sergeant Rhea.'

'I had to act quickly, sir,' I began.

'I appreciate that, but we don't want a panic situation, and we don't want the council criticizing us because we caused them to incur unnecessary overtime payments for their staff . . . so what was your authority for taking action?'

'1947, then 1952.' I realized I had found the magic words and they worked again.

'Right,' he said, seeking no further elaboration. 'Say no more. I'm on my way. Stay there until I arrive, give me fifteen minutes.'

During the next couple of hours or so, things happened with bewildering speed; the office filled with police officers, men and women, who had been summoned to Eltering by radio from Force Control. The police station forecourt seemed suddenly full of police vehicles; a fire service car arrived too with one of their senior officers, council bosses turned up, and within a very short time there was a full-scale operation in progress. During the general discussion led by Inspector Breckon in the police station's muster room, I learned that the council had acted with remarkable speed—they'd had a stock of sandbags already prepared for such emergencies within their area and soon one of their vehicles was heading up to the moors to deposit a large pile of them at the point where the waters would be parted. One of their men knew exactly where to go—he'd done the same trip as a young man in 1952, and although the town centre had been flooded for a time on that occasion, this action had diverted much of the water which arrived later. It had been nothing like 1947. The risk of flooding had continued for almost two weeks and there was no doubt this action had prevented other large-scale floods over that period. It had also allowed the initial flood water to drain away from the town centre earlier than otherwise. The rocky, isolated location of the junction with the old beck meant that a permanent diversion was almost impossible to construct. Sandbags were a practical and suitable compromise, and the diverted flood water would find its way into the main watercourses without any danger to the town or villages.

In 1947, the council had provided sandbags which were placed along the banks of the beck at its most vulnerable point where it flowed through the town centre. That exercise had been repeated in 1952 with council officials knowing the danger points and so, although the beck presently showed no signs of rising or overflowing, those simple precautions were speedily taken. Records still existed in the council files and so the present men knew precisely where to place the bags. This burst of activity along the beckside, with flashing orange lights, rotating blue lights and vehicles using their headlights as torches to guide the workmen, and with two or three police cars in attendance, attracted the interest of people in pubs or walking in the town and so word of a likely flood situation soon spread. The tactics at this early stage were not to order evacuation but to alert householders, shopkeepers and property owners to the possibility of a flood so they could take whatever personal action they considered necessary. Some would sandbag their own doorways, others would lift vulnerable furniture off the floor and stand it on bricks, some would take their worldly possessions upstairs and others would simply sit it out. Evacuation would be a last resort—most of these properties could cope with floods up to two-feet deep without immediate risk to human life.

It was 11.15 before we heard that sandbags had been placed in position higher upstream, but a radio report from the council workmen at the scene confirmed that the water upstream was rising rapidly. Thanks to their prompt action, much of the overflow had been diverted into the old riverbed but even so, a large amount was bypassing the temporary dam and heading down the beck towards Eltering. It was thought our town defences and the culvert could cope with a fairly hefty rise in the water level and so we all felt we had won the race against time. All we could do now was wait.

And wait we did. By midnight, we could see the water was beginning to rise with astonishing speed. At this stage, almost everyone living near the beckside in town, or with properties along its banks, had been made aware of the situation and many of them turned out to watch the rising water. Some brought flasks of hot cocoa or coffee, others were equipped with powerful torches to shine on the water's surface and most wore wellington boots. And then, at twenty past twelve, there was a definite surge in the level of flowing brown water and it began to creep higher up the banks. From our vantage point, we could see it rushing into the culvert which was a huge concrete pipe beneath some buildings and the road. It was about three feet (one metre) in diameter and the roar from it was awe inspiring. The raging water hurtled out of the other end, some twenty yards away and flowed towards the distant river, at the far side of the culvert, the banks were high enough to contain the extra depth. The danger was at the upper end where the mass of downflowing water tried to squeeze into a space which was far too small to take it.

Thanks to local intelligence, we knew that even if it overflowed the banks in the town centre, it would require a further rise of a foot or so before it reached any of the nearby properties and so, without any thought of the passage of time, we all waited and waited. The snag was that none of us had any idea how much water was yet to come from the thawing snow on the distant moors but by 2.30, the water level began to recede. One man thought the chill night air of the uplands had halted the thaw temporarily, but that it would resume if the sun repeated today's temperatures. Almost imperceptibly, therefore, the water level became static and it appeared to have passed its peak.

Nonetheless, it had reached the first layer of sandbags and some water had seeped through, but as we stood around and waited, it was evident it was not going to rise any further. Indeed, as the minutes ticked away, it seemed to be dropping slightly. The consensus was that the crisis was over, at least for tonight. Tomorrow, however, was another day, but it was with some relief that we realized the vital defences were in position and the town was most unlikely to suffer even if there was another rapid thaw tomorrow or later. All the sandbags, both in town and on the moors, would remain in position until the risk was over.

As I drove home, I made a mental note to write a thank-you letter to Arnold Snape and also to thank Alf Ventress for providing me with his magic words, the image of that unforgettable moorland winter of 1947 and the vital lessons learned in 1952.

* * *

As the snow thawed on the moors that March, it caused several other becks and gills to overflow and some rivers reached a worryingly high level although generally this affected little more than fields along their route. There was no large-scale flooding, no evacuation of residents, no blocked roads, no livestock swept away and no bridges washed down—just a lot of water standing around in fields and low-lying areas.

It was during this time that the village policeman at Slemmington received a telephone call from one of his local people and, in my capacity as acting sergeant, I happened to be in his office at the time. Like me, Jim Collins had an office attached to his police house and I had called on him to check some details in a report about a road traffic accident. It was 10.30 one Tuesday morning and we were enjoying a coffee, courtesy of his wife, Lydia. When the phone rang, he responded with, 'Oh, good morning, George. What can I do for you?'

I could hear the male voice at the other end of the line. 'Well, Jim, mebbe it's nowt, but there's a tent in the middle of that field behind Kirkcliff Church. It was surrounded by water when I went past yesterday, the tent I mean, and it's still there, I saw it about an hour ago. It's a bit early for folks to go camping, isn't it?'

'Thanks, I'll have a look,' Jim promised his caller.

And so it was that Jim and I found ourselves heading for Kirkcliff Church, a fascinating eleventh-century building standing beside a small beck, but with no village nearby.

There wasn't even a farm near this old church for it stood literally in the middle of nowhere near a long bend in Kirkcliff Beck.

A few yards downstream, the beck flowed through a gap in a ridge of higher ground; centuries ago, it had probably flowed underground in this limestone region but over the years the tunnel route had been eroded by weather and water to become an open gully. It was these twin cliffs, one at each side of the beck, plus the old church, which gave the locality its name.

Kirkcliff Beck was interesting too. For most of the year, its bed was dry and comprised nothing more than large rounded stones. As this was a limestone region, there were vast underground caverns hereabouts and the water which flowed in the higher reaches of Kirkcliff Beck disappeared underground some two miles upstream. Only if there was heavy rain or rapidly melting snow on the moors did this part of the beck fill with water and even so, it rarely reached the river which lay several miles away—it usually managed to vanish underground at some point. In spite of this disappearing trick, the beck was capable of overflowing in severe weather conditions, and one part which invariably suffered was the field behind Kirkcliff Church. It had never been known, however, for flood waters to reach the old church or the surrounding graveyard, which had been sited wisely on a convenient hillock.

Jim and I arrived separately; each had our own Minivan and I was on my way back to Ashfordly via this location, and so we halted in the small car park beside the church and walked down to the field. We were confronted with what looked like a miniature lake or very large pond with a small green ridge tent standing in the middle, with water rising some three inches up its walls.

The water was not flowing; it had lapped over the banks of the beck at some stage and now flooded the field because it had nowhere else to go. It was standing very still and a pair of mallard were swimming happily near the tent. The field would not be dry again until the water had either evaporated completely or soaked into the ground, and that might take several days or even longer.

'Wellie time!' grinned Jim, and so we returned to our vans, donned wellington boots which we always carried as part of our emergency kit, and returned. As the water was only ankle deep, and the field's base quite solid, we had no difficulty splodging across to the isolated tent. Our concern was that someone might be ill inside—we didn't think the water was deep enough to have caused a drowning.

There was always a possibility, of course, that it had flooded very suddenly and very deeply at some earlier stage, but when I opened the flap, the tent, large enough to accommodate two adults, was almost empty. Inside, a handful of abandoned belongings were floating on the water—the corner of a ground sheet showed as well as a plastic mug, a leather glove, some pieces of newspaper and sticks which looked like fire-lighting materials and one or two other bits and pieces such as a paper plate, the wrapping from a bar of chocolate and an apple.

'What do you reckon?' Jim asked me.

'Somebody was sleeping here when the water rose; he had to abandon ship in a hurry and has decided to leave the tent here until the water has subsided,' I suggested. 'If it happened at night, he'd have no idea how deep the water was going to be; he'd get out while the going was good, taking whatever he could carry.'

'Seems as good an explanation as any, but it's a funny time of year to be camping,' Jim said. 'March isn't the best of months, what with frost, wind, rain and even snow about.'

'We'd better do a more thorough check,' I said, and waddled inside like a duck, squatting on my haunches and hoping I would not overbalance into the water. But there was nothing of interest other than the bits we had already seen. Everything indicated that someone had vacated the tent in a hurry and so we decided there was nothing else we could do, other than to record the fact in our Occurrence

Book. Leaving the tent in its lagoon, Jim left to return to Slemmington while I motored back to Ashfordly Police Station. When I walked in, Alf Ventress was on duty with the place full of smoke and cigarette ash covering the polished counter.

'Vesuvius erupted again, has it, Alf?' I commented, whereupon he swept away the ash with his jacket sleeve. 'Anything else happened?'

'All quiet, Nick, all under control,' he said with practised ease. Alf could persuade everyone that it was all quiet and under control even if a bomb had dropped on the marketplace or there'd been an earthquake under the police station. 'Nothing to report,' he added for good measure.

'No reports of lost tents?' I asked.

'Lost tents?' he frowned. 'Why, has somebody found one?'

'There's one in that field behind Kirkcliff Church,' I told him. 'A green one, ridge style, large enough to sleep two adults. It's deserted, but it's standing in the middle of a large pool of water where the beck's overflowed.'

'Abandoned, you think?'

'It's hard to say, the groundsheet's still there, along with some bits of personal rubbish.'

'So there's no one loitering with intent?' and he chuckled at his own joke. 'Funny thing to leave behind, though, unless he had to get out very quickly.'

'That's what we thought—Jim Collins was with me. It looks as though someone's been sleeping there and the river overflowed, making him abandon things while he could. We'll record it just in case we get more reports.'

'Right you are, Nick, or should I say Sarge,' he smiled. 'I'll put it in the book. But it's a funny time of year to be going camping,' he added. 'I wouldn't have thought anyone would want to sleep out of doors at this time of year, unless they were forced to. Seems like a form of torture to me.'

'Someone kicked out of his home maybe? Rebellious teenager, or erring husband? Somebody on the run even?'

'Somebody on the run,' mused Alf, and I could now see that his mind was turning to something he'd read earlier. 'You know, Nick, you might be on to something there. Did you see that crime report about a fortnight ago? A series of raids on isolated farmhouses, cash stolen in every case, egg money, milk money, money from the farmer's wife's hand-bag, money put out for the insurance man, that sort of thing. Small amounts really, subsistence money almost . . . now, if I can put my hands on that report.'

'Have we had any such reports in our area?' I asked, as Alf started to rummage around his filing system.

'Not to my knowledge. They were spread along the Great North Road, Nick, coming up from the south. The first was somewhere near Huntingdon and there were others in lonely farmhouses near spots like Peterborough, Stamford and Grantham, just as if the thief was heading north day by day and paying his way by pinching from lonely farms. No one ever saw him, he just sneaked in, nicked a few pounds and made off. He didn't break in, he managed to sneak into the farmhouses while the owners were down the fields or out in the buildings. It was thought he'd done other jobs which weren't reported. It was always the same MO; slipped into a farmhouse, made off with a few quid lying about. Some owners mebbe never missed the money.'

'But we're a long way from the Great North Road,' I reminded Alf who was now turning pages and flicking through his collected circulars.

'Yes, but there was a raid near York, and another near Malton, not many days ago, both along the A64 so it seems he's moved away from the Great North and is heading into our part of the world. Some collator had gathered all the data and circulated it in a Regional Crime Supplement. Ah, he we are . . .'

He spread a crime circular in front of me and it listed a whole sequence of small raids as Alf had recounted. In every case, small amounts of loose cash had been taken, no vehicle had been heard, no one had been observed in the vicinity and in a few instances, it was said items of food had been taken too.

Each raid was so similar to the earlier ones that a single culprit, travelling north, was almost a certainty but the thief left no traces, no footprints and certainly no fingerprints.

'Have we been notified of any escaped prisoners on the run?' I asked him. 'Or Borstal absconders?'

He shook his head. 'Not for a long time, Nick. So, it's just a thought. If chummy has been travelling north, living by raiding lonely farms along the A1 and then veering off the Great North Road into our part of the world, you might just have found his lair. If he is travelling by stealing, a tent would seem a logical answer to the question of where he put his head down or managed to hide.'

'You could be right,' I said. 'As you say, camping at this time of year isn't exactly a thing you'd do from choice. So I reckon we should keep an eye on that tent, Alf.'

'He might have abandoned it, Nick; don't forget it might have been stolen too, even if we've not had any reports about it. He might have no further use for it and he could be miles away by now. If he is on the run, he'll know the tent will draw attention to itself especially as it's in the middle of a lake of flood water, and if he's got any sense at all, he won't come back for it. Besides, he might have reached his destination by now.'

'So you reckon it's a waste of time watching the tent?'

'To be honest I do, but we could get all patrolling officers, those on our patch and elsewhere, to keep an eye on it whenever they're passing.'

'I can arrange that,' I said.

'I suppose he could place some value on it.' Alf appeared to be having second thoughts. 'He might have paid good money for it, so he could just come back to retrieve it. Who knows?'

'Who indeed, Alf!'

Deciding that regular observations by patrolling constables was the best course of action, I issued my own circular to all officers in the Ashfordly section, and included those at Brantsford and Eltering. I explained about the tent and its location while asking that patrolling police officers paid regular visits to the site in the hope they might come across someone dealing with it. I also suggested there could be a link with the travelling thief who might now be in our area. It was a few days later when I received a call from a motor patrol officer operating from the Scarborough Road Traffic Division.

'It's PC Charlton,' he announced himself. 'I've just seen your circular on our noticeboard, the one about the tent. We've been keeping our eyes open for an army deserter, Sarge, name of Private Ken Stilton whose home is Scarborough. He deserted about a month ago and was well equipped to live rough, his unit thinks he's heading for home.'

'Well, Kirkcliff isn't far from Scarborough; he could be making an indirect approach if he thinks he's being hunted.'

'His unit's certainly looking for him. He's been sick for some time and wants to be discharged from the army. We've checked his home address regularly but we're certain he's not there. Aldershot military police rang us direct because they said there was no likelihood of him going anywhere else, knowing his state of mind. They're sure he's homebound.'

'Thanks, I'll give them a call, the tent might be known to them.'

I rang Aldershot military police and spoke to a Corporal Grantley who was aware of Stilton's personality—Stilton was only twenty years old—and he confirmed that a green ridge tent without army camouflage, some provisions and cooking utensils had been stolen from the unit at the time of Stilton's disappearance. I now felt sure we knew the identity of the culprit, and told Grantley that we would salvage the tent from its watery site and care for it at Ashfordly Police Station. I suggested that if a military police officer was in the vicinity, he should call and have a look at it, just to make sure it was an army tent and that it had been abandoned by Stilton.

Our rather modest revelations persuaded the military police to concentrate their efforts around the Scarborough area, and we assured them we would also remain alert for sightings of Stilton. If his tent had been erected at Kirkcliff two or three days ago, and he had walked from there towards his home, he must now be very close to seeing his family, unless he was deliberately keeping out of the way until he felt it safe to proceed.

I felt a little sorry for him and felt sure there must be less drastic means of securing one's discharge from the armed forces.

To cut short a long story, one of our town patrols in Scarborough noticed a dishevelled young man lurking around the back of a fish-and-chip shop and, with the aid of a police dog handler who happened to be nearby, the lad was arrested. It was Private Stilton. He was taken to the police station and later handed over to military custody to answer military charges and allegations of larceny from several farm-houses. In spite of the trouble he was due to face, he managed to see his mother before he was taken back to Aldershot. I have often wondered what happened to him.

CHAPTER 3

One of the most hilarious episodes among the snows of that winter concerned that old protagonist, Claude Jeremiah Greengrass. He had spotted an advert in the local *Gazette* which offered for sale a selection of musical instruments and, being something of an entrepreneur, he reckoned that if he bought them cheap, he might be able to sell them at a profit. The selection included a trombone, a double bass, a violin, an oboe and a mouth organ.

The seller was an elderly lady called Freda Donaldson whose late husband had been a keen musician and, following his death, she had decided to dispose of all his instruments, with the exception of his piano; she could play that and therefore decided to keep it as a memento. The rest would be disposed of because she felt someone should be given the chance of playing them, a fate she decided was infinitely better than letting them deteriorate beneath a pile of dust through lack of use.

Mrs Donaldson was a very pleasant arty lady well into her seventies with a penchant for flowing dresses, silk scarves and brightly coloured stockings. She lived in a former farmhouse which was perched literally on the top of Gelderslack Bank. The road up to her home was extremely steep, with a 1-in-3 (33%) gradient for most of its half-mile ascent, and there was a sharp left-hand bend at the bottom as one descended. The local people, accustomed to lots of similar hills throughout the moors, did not find Gelderslack Bank at all daunting even if tourists turned pale at the thought of either ascending or descending. For Mrs Donaldson, who drove a small car, the hill held no terrors at all; she had used it every day of her adult life.

In the early hours of the same Friday that her advert appeared in the paper, there was a very heavy fall of snow with some drifting on the higher ground. Lots of minor roads had been blocked or made impassable—and one of the places rendered almost impassable was Gelderslack Bank. There had been some drifting along the approach lane at the top of the hill but that had not deterred regular drivers of larger vehicles; it was the slippery nature of the steep hill rather than surrounding drifts which presented the real problem. The hill itself had become like glass in spite of liberal gritting, and the result was that nothing could ascend it.

Unfortunately, attempts to descend it were also fraught with danger and the first casualty was a brewery lorry with a load of barrels of beer and bottles in crates. The driver was at the top of the hill, having safely forged his way through the drifts, and although he was very experienced and had coped with most of the notorious descent, he had found himself sliding inexorably downhill on those final yards close to the bottom. He was unable to steer effectively and also unable to brake on the ice. As he had battled with his steering wheel and brakes, he had slithered sideways, his onward dash delayed just a fraction when either his front or rear wheels collided with the high verges as he bounced from one to the other without a hope of halting his rush. His lorry, fortunately not having slid down the entire slope and not moving with any great speed, hit the verge at the bottom corner and overturned into a thick copse of snow-laden shrubs and undergrowth.

Much of his load spilled out and some bottles were smashed but he was not injured, merely highly embarrassed and rather apprehensive about what his boss would say and do.

I was called out to the accident and was wearing my acting sergeant's stripes. As the snow was not particularly deep on the lower roads, I could drive most of the way to the scene even if it meant walking the final yards; then I could decide what action to take. There was no great urgency because the driver was not injured and the road wasn't blocked because the brewery wagon had overturned and was clear of the carriageway. Whether other vehicles would attempt to either climb or descend the hill while the lorry lay there disabled was something I could not determine—one worry was that some other driver might lose control down the hill and collide with the first casualty. Happily, there wasn't much traffic that day.

When I arrived around 10.30, I saw Claude Jeremiah Greengrass's old red truck parked at the foot of the hill, safely away from the carriageway on a patch of waste ground but he was not in attendance, and his dog Alfred was not in the cab either. The truck was facing towards the incline, so I guessed Claude had wanted to climb the hill but had been prevented by the conditions. It seemed he had abandoned his truck temporarily—but where had he gone? At this point, I knew nothing about the musical instruments being for sale at the house on top of the hill—that was something I discovered later.

The lorry driver, who came from Hartlepool in County Durham, explained how he had got himself into this predicament. Fortunately he had a flask of coffee in the cab—undamaged, and I suggested he had a drink immediately because a hot sweet drink was a good antidote to shock in these circumstances. As he sipped—I declined his offer of a mouthful—we took stock of the situation. We decided that a breakdown truck with heavy lifting gear was necessary but probably not until the carriageway of the hill was free from snow. We realized, too, that another brewery wagon was required to remove the undamaged load, and that should not be called until the roads were clear. The necessary and fairly routine action for dealing with the accident soon got underway and, happily, the snow on the road surfaces in the lower parts of the dale began to thaw where the sun touched it, even if it was not doing so on the heights, nor indeed on Gelderslack Bank.

It was while talking to the lorry driver at the foot of the hill that I became aware of someone walking down and after a moment or two saw who it was—it was Claude Jeremiah Greengrass accompanied by Alfred. But Claude was carrying a massive object and, as the lorry driver and myself halted our conversation to observe this curious arrival, I saw his load was a double bass. The size and shape was distinctive, even if it was encased in its strong wooden cover, painted black. Claude was finding it very difficult to keep to his feet and it was inevitable that both I and the lorry driver, whose name was Stan, stood and watched.

In those first moments, I don't think Claude realized he had an audience, nor do I believe he knew that the lorry had come to grief at the bottom of the hill; his entire concentration was upon keeping his feet and that was complicated due to the size, shape, weight and sheer ungainliness of the bass.

'He's going to lose it . . .' Stan said. 'He's going to slip and if he does, he'll slide right down here. God knows what'll happen to that thing he's carrying!'

'Claude!' I shouted, in a vain hope of persuading him not to attempt this impossible journey with the bass. 'Claude, don't try and cope with this steep bit, it's sheet ice under the snow, it's like glass . . .'

He didn't hear me, or if he did, he pretended not to and then he spotted us. By this stage, he had progressed with moderate success and was about a third of the way down the hill, but by no means on to the steepest and most slippery part. I tried shouting again but he could not hear me— there was a slight breeze blowing and perhaps it was stronger even at that modest height—and onwards he came. Then he saw the overturned beer wagon some distance below and the surprise, fear even, was evident because he halted in his tracks. Or rather, he tried to.

As he attempted to halt, his feet slipped from under him. Both feet slid forward together on that snow-covered, glass-like icy surface and he sat down with an almighty bump, landing heavily on his backside and, in that split second, he lost his grip on the double bass. It fell away and even though he was already sliding slowly down the hill on his rump, he made a huge lunge forward to try and seize the instrument as it moved steadily away from him.

But the strong wooden cover of the double bass was ideal for sliding down sheet ice and it shot away from him as he made a final desperate attempt to grab it. He managed to seize the part which contained the slender neck—the wooden case was shaped to accommodate it—but by this stage, Claude was lying on his stomach with arms outstretched and clinging to the bass as if his life depended upon it.

There was nothing we could do but stand and watch this piece of impromptu entertainment as Alfred trotted along behind as if this was a perfectly normal event. It was at such moments that I wished I had a camera with me. Stan and I were then treated to the sight of a massive double bass lying on its back as it whizzed down the ice and snow-covered slope with Claude Jeremiah Greengrass hanging on to it for dear life with legs flailing and his hoarse voice calling, 'Help me, you daft bats . . . get up here and stop this thing . . .'

The only way we could have stopped the onward descent of both the heavy bass and the sliding Claude was to stand in the road in the vain hope we could divert either or both or slow down their hectic progress, but that was fraught with danger. For one thing it was impossible to stand on the steepest and most slippery part, and secondly, neither Stan nor I had any wish to be knocked over by this oncoming guided weapon. Not that there was much guidance being deployed! There was so little time to do anything either; rather, it was a case of Claude hanging on while he and his instrument hurtled ever onwards and downwards.

The camber on the road allowed him to effect a good cornering manoeuvre because the bass went into the turn almost like one of those high-speed Olympic toboggans with Claude still hanging on behind and Alfred making good use of the verges to gallop alongside where there was virgin snow. By this stage, however, a considerable turn of speed had been developed by both man and bass and instead of following the route of the road, the bass, looking rather like a boat being swept down a waterfall, sailed upwards on the bend and shot over the rim with Claude still holding on.

With an immense crash of branches, a good deal of cursing and showers of soft new snow being thrown in all directions, Claude and the bass came to rest in the undergrowth behind the brewery lorry. Alfred arrived seconds later and began to lick Claude's face with Claude shouting, 'Gerr off, you silly hound!'

As Stan and I ran to do what we could, Claude struggled to his feet covered in ice, snow and broken twigs and his first words were, 'All right, all right, have a good laugh. I could have killed himself there . . . you never told me the hill was like a skating rink.'

'Are you hurt, Claude?' was my concern.

'Not me; it'll take more than a bit of ice and snow to get through this coat of mine, I reckon it'll even keep bullets out, but what about that bass . . .'

And he hobbled back into the undergrowth to haul out the huge case. One or two bits of wood had been knocked from the case to leave some bare patches, but once he had hauled it from the undergrowth, he laid it on the ground where we stood.

He flicked the catches and the big case opened easily. Happily, the massive instrument inside appeared to have survived without damage.

'Claude, if it's not a rude or silly question, what on earth are you doing with a double bass on Gelderslack Bank in conditions like this?'

'I've just bought it, that's what, and I couldn't get my truck up the hill so I walked up to Mrs Donaldson's to pick it up, and I've some more things waiting. It wasn't as slippery as this when I walked up there!'

'Well, it's like a skating rink now. You're not thinking of doing a repeat performance for us, are you?' I laughed.

'Not with a trombone I'm not!' he said. 'Well, I must be off, I'll get this home and then come back when it's cleared up. Anyway, what are you doing here, Constable?'

'You mean who hadn't noticed that lorry?'

'I had, but there's nowt you can do, is there? You need a heavy lifting breakdown truck.'

'It's on its way,' I assured him. 'I'm just glad we didn't have to count you as one of the casualties.'

Stan smiled and said to Claude, 'Do you like beer?'

'I've been known to enjoy a pint or two,' smiled Claude. 'Why?'

'Well, it's amazing, the things that fall off the backs of lorries and there's a crate over there for you, as a thank you for brightening up my day. My bosses allow me to give thank-yous on occasions—so it's for you, with my compliments.'

'Are you staying here long?' beamed Claude at the gesture. 'Because if you are, I might just go back up there for that trombone!'

'Don't you dare, Claude!' I shook a finger at him. 'Wait until we've got this beer lorry moved first. I don't want to cope with you and a trombone, it all sounds far too risky for me. One big fiddle with Greengrass is enough for one day.'

And so ended a curious morning at the bottom of Gelderslack Bank.

* * *

'Greengrass is up to something,' Oscar Blaketon, now owner of the local pub, hailed me, as I walked along the village street some time after that incident. It was a fine morning and he was sweeping the forecourt of his newly purchased premises. Clearly eager for a chat, he halted and leaned on the brush, then looked as if he was prepared to spend all day doing little else. He reminded me of a roadman at work while waiting for his tea-break.

'You'll have to find out what's going on,' he added. 'I don't trust that man, not one single inch.'

'What's he up to exactly, Sarge, to make you so concerned?' I found it difficult to avoid calling Blaketon by his former rank and it was even more difficult using his Christian name. The name Sarge slipped out almost automatically, but I told myself this was no longer my boss giving orders; Blaketon was now a member of the public who was currently passing useful intelligence to the constabulary and it was my responsibility to determine the value of his crime-busting information.

'Search me!' He shrugged his shoulders. 'But I know he's up to something and if previous behaviour is anything to go by, it'll be dodgy to say the least and probably unlawful.'

'So what makes you think he's up to no good?' I pressed him for the reason behind his concern.

'He wants all my empty beer cans,' Blaketon told me. 'He comes with his truck and carries them off by the sackful. Now, I ask you, why would anyone want empty beer cans?'

'They're no good, are they?' I frowned. 'I thought you'd be glad to get rid of them, they only smell and attract flies if they're left outside, children play football with them and they're no good for anything else. If Greengrass is happy to take them off your hands, I would have thought you'd welcome it.'

'Yes, I do, they can be a nuisance when they're left lying around, but what's he up to, Nick? What is he doing with hundreds of empty beer cans? Nobody else has found a use for them, so why does he want as many as I can let him have?'

'Have you asked him?'

'Of course I've asked him, and he told me it was some secret invention he was working on . . . you don't think he would tell me the truth, do you?'

'No, he'd pull your leg at the least, or spin you some unlikely yarn, especially if he knew he'd got you wondering about his behaviour. You're not charging him for them, are you?'

'I'm not, they cost him nothing. I'm glad to get rid of them; he can have as many as he wants for as often as he wants, but it doesn't stop me wondering what he's doing with them.'

'Well, I've no idea, I've not been up to his ranch recently and he's never told me about any new enterprise,' I had to admit. 'But I'll keep an eye open and see what I come up with. I'll let you know if I solve the mystery.'

He thanked me and we had a chat about his new life and the problems he might have to face, and then I had to take my leave because I was due to meet a local farmer within the next few minutes to deal with the renewal of his firearm certificate. As I walked to the farm in question, which was situated a mere half-mile away at the eastern end of the village, I pondered over this new initiative from Greengrass. Although I tried to produce some logical reason why Greengrass would want to encumber himself with hundreds of empty beer cans, I failed.

There were, I knew, lots of things one could do with empty beer bottles but old metal cans did not have the same appeal. The breweries wanted their bottles back and were prepared to expend time, effort and even small rewards to ensure their return, consequently that catered for many of the empty ones. Some people kept their old wine and beer bottles, or even jam jars, and built them into walls both indoors and in their gardens. It was very fashionable at the time and lots of public houses constructed modern internal walls which incorporated empty bottles. This was done to create interesting features with varieties of light, shade and colour, very effective if a light source shone through.

Some collectors even hoarded old bottles because rare specimens could bring good money, and I knew one man who formed the edges of his lawn by pushing green wine bottles into the ground along the extremities, but later he found himself having to be ultra-careful whenever he cut the grass. Boys would even use bottles perched on walls as targets for their catapult practice, or even for potting with air rifles.

I could not imagine anyone wanting to decorate their house or garden with empty beer cans, however, nor did I believe they had yet reached the status of being collectors' items or worth good sums of money. I did not think Greengrass had produced a scheme for recycling them by selling them to gullible people, although, of course, it was quite feasible that young lads with airguns and catapults might want lots of old cans for target practice. But I knew they would not be prepared to pay Greengrass for them when they could collect them by the bagful free from the back door of any public house or licensed restaurant. So, once again, if Blaketon was to be believed, Claude Jeremiah Greengrass was threatening to become a nuisance to the law-abiding citizens of Aidensfield, but how?

I decided not to make a special investigative journey to the Greengrass ranch because that would merely create suspicion in Claude's mind and if he was involved in anything remotely devious, his immediate reaction would be to conceal his endeavours and deny anything that might involve him in a confrontation with the law. If I was to learn his secret, I had to be cautious and cunning; I had to keep my ears and eyes wide open and my senses alert to any new Greengrass scheme.

I wondered if I should call my mission 'Operation Greengrass' to give it some kind of stature—or even 'Operation Beer Can.' That added just a little mystique, I felt.

For the two days following my chat with Blaketon, I was off duty, those being my weekly rest days, and on the day I returned to work I had to attend Eltering Magistrates' Court as a witness in a careless driving prosecution, and the day after that I was earmarked for special duty in Ashfordly for a visit of a travelling circus. It meant, therefore, that I did not have an early opportunity to investigate Blaketon's concerns, nor did I have any reason for visiting Greengrass at home among his piles of assorted junk. Then Blaketon hailed me again.

'Ah, Nick, I don't want to be a nuisance, but have you discovered anything about Greengrass and those beer cans?'

'Sorry, Sarge, not yet,' and I explained I'd been otherwise engaged for the past few days. 'It's on my list of things to do, but I don't want to scare him off by showing too much interest in his activities. I thought the softly-softly approach was best.'

'I couldn't agree more, but there's been a development I thought you should know.'

'What sort of development?' This was getting even more intriguing.

'He's been buying crates of beer,' Blaketon said, and the lowering of his tone of voice suggested there was something very illegal about it. Which there wasn't. Anyone could buy crates of beer provided they obeyed the various rules and regulations imposed by the liquor licensing laws.

'Crates of beer?' I must have sounded puzzled by this revelation.

'Lots of them,' Blaketon added with a hint of suggested unlawfulness. 'I've lost count but it's too many for himself to drink even in a couple of months.'

'It sounds as if he's going to have a party.' This seemed the most logical solution. 'Is it his birthday or something?'

'No, it isn't, so there you are, Nick. Another sign of impending trouble, mark my words.'

'But if someone else had come in and bought a few crates of beer from you, you'd have been delighted, Sarge. It's quite normal, people buy it in crates for weddings, parties, private functions of every kind. I see nothing to concern us in that, to be honest.'

'Not even when he's still taking away dozens of empty beer cans?'

'You don't think he's pouring the beer into the cans, resealing them and then re-selling it at a profit, do you? With his own name on them?' I smiled at the unlikely idea.

'I wouldn't put it past that man, Nick, in fact I wouldn't put anything past him. But there you are, two unlikely activities in a very short space of time from one of our most notorious rogues. It adds up to something, Nick, he's being extremely devious and he knows I'm intrigued; he's trying to keep it from me. Now, if I was still in my uniform and in charge of Ashfordly section, I'd be sending you up there to his hovel to sniff around, to find out what's going on.'

'I can't see anything remotely illegal in what he's been doing, Sarge,' I had to say. 'And I've no authority to go snooping on him or poking around his premises.'

'This is not an ordinary person we're dealing with, Nick, this is Greengrass remember!'

There had always been an element of personal antagonism between Blaketon and Greengrass but no one knew the reason; now, it seemed, it was destined to continue even while Blaketon was no longer a serving police officer. It occurred to me, however, that Greengrass might be doing nothing more than creating a bizarre set of circumstances for no other reason than to excite the curiosity of his old adversary. As Blaketon showed an increasing curiosity about the affair, so Greengrass would perform other acts merely to tease or annoy him. Greengrass had the proverbial carrot which he was dangling before a donkey, i.e. Blaketon.

'I'll check it out, Sarge,' I promised. 'But I know you'll appreciate it has to be low priority. But as I said before, I'll let you know what I discover.'

A couple of days later, I had to visit the Greengrass ranch. The CID at Force Headquarters had received intelligence from the West Riding Constabulary to the effect that a team of confidence tricksters from Leeds was in the area preying on elderly people living in isolated country homes, and so I had to tour my patch to warn possible victims. And Claude, being a pensioner of indeterminate age who lived in a remote house, clearly matched the profile of a potential victim. This provided me with a very sound reason to pay a call.

I drove my little police van down the rough pot-hole ridden track to his untidy spread and, as I parked it away from patches of mud, Alfred, his flea-ridden lurcher came bounding from one of the outbuildings, barking and creating a huge fuss. He was followed by his lord and master who ambled out to see what was happening, then halted when he saw me. I disembarked and went across to him.

'Good afternoon, Claude, not a bad day for the time of year,' I greeted him.

'It was all right until you showed up,' he grunted. 'So what is it now? What am I supposed to have done, because whatever it is, I didn't do it and I was nowhere near at the time.'

'I'm not here to quiz you, Claude, I'm here to warn you against some con men from Leeds; they're supposed to be in our area, conning elderly folks . . .'

'Elderly folks? Why are you coming here then? I'm not elderly, I'm still a working man, still earning my keep, not like some I could mention.'

'They're concentrating on isolated properties, Claude, pretending to fix loose tiles on roofs or clear gutters and downpipes, and then they'll charge you a fortune for work that is sub-standard or not done at all.'

'I thought everybody was like that,' he chuckled. 'So you expect me to fall for a con man's story? Come on, Constable Nick, you know me better than that. No slippery tongued con man is going to get one over me, and as for fixing roofs and gutters there's nobody better than me around here. I can fix my own.'

'We're warning everyone, Claude, so if they do come here, perhaps you would let me know? We like to keep track of them, and maybe you could get their vehicle registration number, a telephone number or even a name and address.'

'You want me to do your job as well as my own, eh?' he grinned. 'But thanks, if they come here, I'll deal with 'em, make no mistake about it. Two can play at their game; I might even sell 'em something useless, eh?'

'Like old beer cans?' I couldn't resist the remark and I had spoken it almost before I realized.

'Beer cans?' he frowned.

Now committed, I waded in with, 'I heard on the grape-vine that you've been collecting empty beer cans.'

He grinned wickedly.

'Blaketon been talking, has he? There should be confidentiality between a pub landlord and his customers, like there is between somebody confessing to a priest or between a solicitor and a client.'

'He told me, during a conversation about something else, that he was glad you were taking away his empty beer cans. You're providing useful service, he says.'

'Does he now?' and Claude's eyes revealed he was enjoying his battle with Blaketon. 'And I'll bet he asked you to come snooping, to find out what I was doing with 'em? He's dying to know, Constable; he keeps asking why I want them, and I'm not saying, I just keep going back for more. So that's why you're here, is it? To see what I'm doing with my beer cans?'

'No, I came to offer you some good crime prevention advice.'

'And pigs might fly! Look, Constable Rhea, it wouldn't surprise me if Blaketon's told you about those crates of beer I bought, or those cloakroom tickets from the post office, and that megaphone I've borrowed from the secretary of Aidensfield Show.'

'Cloakroom tickets? No, he's not mentioned those! Or the megaphone.'

'Then he will, Constable, he will. Now, you've done your bit, you've warned me about some villains and I'm grateful, but now I've things to do. Busy people can't spend time standing around all day talking to the law. So goodbye.'

And he turned and walked back into the outbuilding with Alfred at his heels. I could see that he was grinning widely and realized he had scored some kind of victory over Blaketon.

Later that day I popped into Blaketon's pub, in uniform and on an official visit, when he asked, 'Nick, I don't suppose you've had a chance to visit Greengrass?'

'As a matter of fact I have,' I smiled. 'Officially too. I was warning him and others about some Leeds con men who are operating in this area.'

'They'll meet their match if they come here and try to con me, but did you manage to find out what he's up to?'

'Only that he's been buying cloakroom tickets from the post office,' I smiled. 'And a megaphone from the show secretary. I wondered if he was going to use them in conjunction with those beer cans and crates of beer.'

'A megaphone? And cloakroom tickets? He's not going to raffle the beer, is he?'

'Sarge, I've no idea what he intends doing with all those things, but there's no sign of anything happening or being organized at his ranch. As I said, I'll keep my ears to the ground, my eyes open and my curiosity well tuned.'

I left Blaketon to his worries about Greengrass and did a quick tour of the neighbouring pubs to carry out routine checks, warning people about the con men as I travelled around, and booked off duty at ten that evening without discovering the Greengrass secret. As I enjoyed a late supper with Mary, I found myself pondering Greengrass's activity and decided it must be something to do with a show-type event of some kind—the megaphone suggested he was to address a large crowd in the open air and the cloakroom tickets indicated a raffle. Lots of local people who arranged small raffles made good use of books of cloakroom tickets printed in various colours and these were quite legal in specific cases. Such raffles were known, in legal terms, as small lotteries which were incidental to certain entertainments such as bazaars, sales-of-work, dinners, dances, sporting events and similar occasions, and there were some modest rules. I could advise Greengrass about those rules if the occasion arose.

The crates of beer, which he was not allowed to sell but which could be given away, suggested an event of some kind too, one with a lot of thirsty men taking part. Perhaps the beer was some kind of inducement? But the empty beer cans? That remained a puzzle.

I must admit I wondered if Greengrass was doing all this simply to score points over Blaketon, but, on reflection, his activity seemed rather too grand for a mere joke and it was unlike Greengrass to invest his own precious cash merely to bait anyone. Those crates of beer alone must have cost him a few pounds.

The next day, however, the whole affair was revealed. It was a Saturday in May and the date of the Elsinby Spring Show. As I was on duty and that village was on my beat, I had to attend, both to patrol the showground and to deal with traffic both entering and leaving. The showfield was called John's Field, the memorial to a local tramp who had lived in the village. It was spacious enough to accommodate the entire panoply of an agricultural show from livestock to crafts by way of exhibitions of flowers and other spring produce. Lots of exhibitors were expected, including some local trade stands, and there would be refreshments, competitions and races for the children, a dog show, a pet show and demonstrations of equestrian skills, sheep dogs in action and hound trailing with much more to entertain and educate the visitors.

And then, as I wandered around the showfield before the gates were opened to the public, I spotted Greengrass. He had his own display—a large untidily written sign announced 'Greengrass Shooting Gallery' with a note saying 'Ten shots for half-a-crown, valuable prizes.' I couldn't resist a peep at this attraction and when I entered his compound, Alfred barked and Greengrass appeared from the tent which formed the shelter for him and his equipment.

'Now then, Constable,' he chuckled. 'We're not open yet but you can have a privileged go . . . only half-a-crown for ten shots. Thre'pence a go.'

'And how do I win my prize?'

'If you score ten direct hits, you win.'

'Ten out of ten, you mean?'

'Aye, a full house. You have to score a full house to win.'

'And what do I win?'

'A bottle of beer,' he grinned.

'And when I pay my money, I get one half of a cloak-room ticket and join the queue for my turn?'

'By gum, you're sharp today, Constable. But you're right.'

'And what do I shoot at?'

'Beer cans,' he grinned. 'Empty beer cans provided by Oscar Blaketon, free of charge.'

'You don't mean they're all lined up on a wall, do you?'

'Not so simple as that, Constable Nick, not so simple at all! Here, let me show you summat,' and he led me into the tent and lifted up a metal device which looked rather like the base of the torch used to light the Olympic flame. It was surprisingly heavy but had a slender handle beneath and a round flat surface on top, with lots of other mysterious things in between.

'This is a target launcher,' he explained. 'It's a simplified miniature hand-held version of the machine that sends clay pigeons into the air. You put your beer can on that plate on the top,'—and he patted a small round plate—'then you aim it into the air, well away from buildings and people, and press the trigger.'

'And it fires the can into the air, is that it?'

'Right first time. It's loaded with one .22 blank and it sends the can sixty feet into the air. I make sure it's aimed over there, towards that wood, and when it's all over, I collect the litter. I'm very responsible you see, Constable, I'm not a vandal and I'm not breaking the law.'

'Well, thanks for telling me all that; at least it's solved Blaketon's query!' I laughed, wondering whether the patent launcher qualified as a firearm but I decided to ignore the legalities.

'You'll be having a go?' he laughed.

'Not today, Claude. I've got other things to do right now, the gates are due to open any minute and I've traffic to see to.'

And so I left Claude to play with his new toy. It was a few days later when I encountered Blaketon once again. I was pleased to explain Claude's need for empty beer cans, a need which had now expired, and Blaketon nodded.

'Well, thanks for that, Nick, at least I know what he was doing with my old cans. The trouble with Greengrass is that you never know what he's up to. Now, I don't want to be a nuisance, but you might be interested in his latest venture.'

'Latest venture?' I puzzled.

'Yes, he's asked me if I can let him have six dozen tri-angular shaped beermats, and I've heard he's been asking at the shop for six dozen clothes pegs and seven extra-large-sized dog collars. He's also looking for the rear part of a lorry exhaust pipe and a pair of rams' horns. What do you think he's up to this time?'

'I'll let you sort that one out,' I laughed.

CHAPTER 4

No one in Aidensfield could understand why Walter Plumpton, a sturdy, balding and rather dour widower in his late forties, a pig farmer by profession and a member of the parish council, suggested a beauty contest for the girls of the district. Much to the surprise of those attending the February parish council meeting, he rose to his feet to put forward his proposal. It was true that Walter was known far and wide as an expert judge of moorland ewes, heavy horses, large white pigs, pet rabbits, potatoes and giant leeks, and that he had more than a brief knowledge of most other forms of livestock and horticultural produce, but no one suspected he might also have a keen and critical eye for the marvels and mysteries of the human female form.

'Precisely what sort of contest are you proposing?' asked the chairman, Rudolph Burley, a local auctioneer. 'This has caught us rather by surprise.'

'Well, summat with lots of lovely girls in it,' beamed Walter, his eyes shining brightly with his enthusiasm. 'In swimming costumes. Parading up and down the side of Ashfordly swimming pool, all smiles and gracefulness and saying how they'd like to change the world or go travelling or just be happy.'

I was attending the meeting in my capacity of village constable. We were encouraged to attend parish council meetings so that any questions involving our duties and work might be answered on the spot. We could not take part in discussing council matters but for many rural bobbies, it was a highly effective means of keeping in touch with matters affecting a village and its people. Our presence was especially valuable as it enabled council members to put questions and concerns directly to us. As just one of several members of the public in attendance, therefore, I listened with some interest to the council's response to Walter's idea.

'I'm not sure about that!' was Councillor Mrs Ramsbottom's immediate response. 'Half-naked young women parading themselves before goggling old men and giggling lads. It's not very seemly, not in my opinion. I don't think many people would approve of such a thing in Aidensfield.'

'They parade half-naked anyway when they use Ashfordly swimming pool!' snapped Walter. 'I can't see any difference between going swimming and walking around t'edge of t'pool as they have to do to get into t'water, or being lined up in t'same place in t'same sort of dress and being judged for, what's t'word, deportment and elegance and intelligence, or whatever. I reckon yon swimming pool's t'best place for a thing like that. It's just a case of organizing all them lovely lasses into a parade of some sort, then finding somebody sensible to judge 'em.'

'I disagree,' persisted Mrs Ramsbottom. 'There's a big difference between going swimming for fun or exercise, and parading half-naked to deliberately flaunt the bits men like to look at, clothed or not, and then be judged like a prize cow. Beauty contests are like cattle markets, no decent young woman would ever demean herself by taking part in such a parade of bare flesh with all the lurid suggestiveness that goes with it. I know I would never have done so.'

'Quite,' smiled Rudolph from his chairman's chair, quietly regarding the rather large and shapeless outline of the fifty-five-year-old grey-haired grandmother. 'But perhaps

Walter has a point. Maybe as representatives of the community, we should consider more interesting means of drawing attention to our village and its assets. Vegetable shows and sheep sales don't attract many folks from afar, so if we staged a beauty contest and opened it to lasses from other villages and from Ashfordly an' all, we might achieve summat worthwhile, summat that would profit our community.'

'You men are all the same!' huffed and puffed Mrs Ramsbottom. 'You think of only one thing. You've got filthy minds . . . it's disgusting, quite disgusting to contemplate. Lots of near naked young women parading around with next-to-nothing on in front of rows of ogling old men and grinning louts . . . and for what, I ask you?'

'For the title of Miss Aidensfield,' beamed Walter. 'With a cup as a prize and mebbe some cash if we can raise some sponsorship, and one of them sashes you drape over their shoulders, and mebbe, if we can find other competitions, our winner could go forward to a bigger contest, like Miss North Yorkshire Moors or Miss North-east Coast, or summat. Even Miss Heather Bell, Miss England even, or Miss World—we've got some bonny lasses in this village, you know, they could really put us on t'map.'

'I don't think true Aidensfieldonians would want to be put on that sort of a map! Or any sort of a map,' snorted Mrs Ramsbottom. 'And most certainly not in the pornographic way you are suggesting. It is demeaning to womanhood and I will not give my consent to such a thing.'

'I am sure the local papers and radio stations would be interested, even television,' mused Rudolph. 'You know, this might be just the thing to bring in tourists, and if we get on to the tourist map it means our local businesses will benefit—the shops and pubs and so forth. We could initiate the idea, and get other villages to do the same, then have a grand finale for the title of Miss Moorland or Queen of the Heather or something else on the lines Walter has suggested . . . with a big prize, lots of publicity . . . yes, Walter, you might have given us something exciting to look forward to. A beauty contest in Aidensfield, eh? It does have a certain appeal.'

'Mr Burley, you're as bad as the rest of them!' snapped Mrs Ramsbottom. 'I never thought I'd hear you voice your support for something with such suggestive undertones.'

'Clearly we need a consensus,' beamed Rudolph. 'I therefore suggest we take a show of hands. At this early stage, all we need is approval to consider the idea in greater depth; if approval for that is given, then we can arrange a feasibility study with a sub-committee to examine the best way to proceed, bearing in mind the best venue and date, possible contests being staged in neighbouring villages, the prizes, the age of the contestants, names of judges and so forth.'

Sitting quietly among the bemused onlookers, I could see by the expression on the faces of the councillors that the idea would receive overwhelming support. After all, Mrs Ramsbottom was the only woman council member apart from the clerk who had no vote; the other six were all men and I could see the happiness of anticipation in their faces.

Rudolph was in firm command of the situation. 'Right,' he said with all the authority of his office. 'I need a proposal. Walter?'

'Aye, right,' said Walter. 'Well, like I said, I propose that Aidensfield stages a beauty contest, with the finer details to be worked out in due course.'

'A seconder?' asked Rudolph, and several hands were shown. 'Jim Preston,' he told the clerk.

'All in favour?' and every hand was shown—except that of Mrs Rambottom.

'Carried,' beamed Rudolph, and so the business of organizing Aidensfield's first beauty contest began in earnest. A sub-committee of three members was appointed with powers to co-opt assistance from anyone experienced in the skills of arranging such an event, and they were also empowered to suggest similar local contests in neighbouring villages with a grand finale in Ashfordly.

Before ending the discussion, Rudolph ventured to suggest that if other villages did enter the spirit of the occasion, any possible grand finale could be held at Ashfordly swimming pool. It was the ideal venue, he reckoned, particularly on a hot summer day. And so the meeting drew to a conclusion with all other subjects under discussion being forgotten. Walter went home looking extremely happy.

I left to continue my patrol as the male council members adjourned to the pub to further consider and discuss this idea. The outcome of that highly informal discussion, which spread to members of the public enjoying a pint or two at the bar, was, of course, that before morning, almost everyone in the village was aware of the plans. Very soon, it became the chief, and indeed only, topic of local conversation.

It is fair to say that the hearts of lots of young girls began to flutter at the thought of winning a beauty competition, while the hearts of their mums began to thump with something approaching trepidation and alarm, perhaps even tinged with a hint of jealousy, while the young men, middle-aged men and indeed old men all warmed to the idea of a parade of lovely young women in scanty bathing costumes. It did not take long for the surrounding villages to emulate Aidensfield by planning their own beauty contests, each with claims that their bonny young lasses were the most beautiful on the planet. As the tempo increased and enthusiasm soared, a scheme developed whereby eleven villages around Ashfordly would each stage their own competition with a grand finale at Ashfordly swimming pool on the last Saturday in August. That finale would comprise twelve girls—Ashfordly would also stage its own Miss Ashfordly contest to bring the number up to twelve—the other girls being the winners of each village contest. A panel of distinguished judges would award the title of Miss Heather Belle to the outright winner, and there would be a cash prize of £100, a guaranteed appearance on local television and a weekend in London.

Various local businesses had offered sponsorship provided their names were given due prominence during the entire proceedings, a keen committee had been formed with the sole responsibility of organizing the event and already it was attracting the interest of the media. And so it was that the Miss Heather Belle competition got underway, thanks to the initiative of Walter Plumpton.

It was during the excitement generated by the preliminary planning that I met Walter as he strolled along Aidensfield main street towards the post office.

He stopped for a chat during which I said, 'That idea of yours has certainly caught the imagination of the area,' I said. 'Everywhere I go, villages are staging competitions and the talk is all about beauty queens and hair styles and bathing suits . . .'

'Aye,' he smiled. 'It's t'mums, you know, they're t'ones pushing their daughters into entering, just as I thought would happen. They're not all like poor old Mrs Ramsbottom, they all think their own lass is t'prettiest for miles around and want t'world to know it. I just hope we finish up with no one scratching eyes out or calling each other names. Some women can get carried away . . . but we're a calm lot up here on t'moors. Anyroad, Mr Rhea, it's all been a bit of good fun so far. You'll be coming to our own competition?'

'Miss Aidensfield. In the village hall, yes. I'll be there,' I assured him.

'Look out for young Susie Buchanan.' He smiled rather secretly. 'I reckon she'll beat the lot!'

'Is there betting on this?' I laughed. 'I'm surprised Greengrass hasn't been offering odds!'

'If he has, I know nowt about it, it's just I've seen yon lass about the place and she's gorgeous . . . really pretty, walks well, talks well, smiles a lot, lovely face and figure . . .'

'I can't say I know her,' I had to admit.

'She's still at school,' he told me. 'Strensford Grammar School. She's sixteen so you might not have seen her around.'

'At her age, she's hardly likely to visit the pub or get involved with anything that comes my way,' I smiled. 'But I'll look out for her. You know her, do you?'

'It's her mother I know. She's a widow; they've got a small market garden along the Elsinby Road. She sells plants and pet animals. I've seen the lass knocking about the place sometimes but can't say I know her very well.'

'Ah, that Buchanan!' I knew the spread to which he referred. I'd had to renew Mrs Buchanan's firearm certificate and shotgun certificate some time earlier. She needed the weapons to keep down vermin on her land and I'd helped her to transfer the documents into her name following the unexpectedly early death of her husband. Mrs Buchanan had taken over the running of their market garden after his death and seemed to be making a very good job of it. 'She's a very nice woman, Mrs Buchanan,' I added.

'She is,' smiled Walter, and I could see a faint flush of embarrassment beginning to creep up his neck and cheeks. I think Walter realized he might have said more than he'd intended, even without using the necessary words, and so he took his leave and I smiled as he continued his way along the street. As I walked away, I wondered about Walter's evident interest in Susie, or was he really fascinated by Mrs Buchanan? She was about his age, possibly a few years younger and very attractive. He, on the other hand, was rather dour and serious, but he was a widower with no children of his own. I'd never seen Walter and Mrs Buchanan together in the village, nor had I come across any situation where they had been with one another elsewhere such as the cinema in Ashfordly or one of the local restaurants.

So far as I knew, Walter was not a regular caller at her market garden—it seemed there was no romance here, unless, of course, it was all one-sided and locked in the mind of Walter Plumpton. But how did that involve young Susie, a schoolgirl of sixteen? And so I found myself with an intriguing question on my mind: had the presence of the lovely young Susie somehow prompted Walter to suggest a beauty contest? If so, why?

There might have been a clue in the fact that Walter turned down an invitation to be one of the judges for the Miss Aidensfield contest. As he'd told the organizing committee,

'Ah'm a good judge of pigs and sheep, and very good with veg-etable produce, fruit and flowers of all kinds, but not lasses. So count me out. Ah'll not be wanting to express my opinion on leggy young women in bathing suits, that's best left to others.'

So the competition went ahead without its prime motivator being involved in any way. Walter was just like the rest of us, an interested bystander without any official duties and even though, at the last minute, the chairman of judges tried to recruit him to their panel, Walter politely but firmly refused, and on a Saturday afternoon in July, the Miss Aidensfield competition was staged in the village hall.

The age of the contestants had been determined as ranging from fifteen up to twenty-five; they had to either have been born in Aidensfield, or to live or work within the parish boundary, and they had to parade before the judges in one-piece swimsuits and court shoes. There would be a pre-determined routine to follow as they walked across the stage, then they would have to answer a few questions about themselves. Great care was taken by the organizers to ensure that the competition was fair to all. After scrutiny by the judges (a team of five, of which two were women) the win-ner would be declared 'Miss Aidensfield' and she would be entered automatically into the Miss Heather Belle competi-tion to be staged at Ashfordly in August.

The Miss Aidensfield event attracted fourteen hopefuls, amongst whom was Susie Buchanan. I went along to watch. The event was popular, for the village hall was packed to capacity and the WI had laid on tea and drinks after the contest. It was very well organized—the girls prepared them-selves in the dressing-rooms behind the stage and the judges sat to one side of the stage in full view of the audience. The girls entered one by one, having drawn lots for their turns, walked a pre-determined route around the stage so that the judges and audience could see them, cheer them, applaud them and whistle at them, and then, before lining up at the side of the stage opposite the judges, each girl was asked five questions, one from each of the judges. Marks were awarded for their entire performance and appearance. It had been decided there would be no second or third prizes—the organizers felt it better to declare a single winner which, in their view, meant that all the other girls were equal as runners-up.

As I observed the show, I spotted Walter in a seat close to the front, then saw he was sitting directly behind Mrs Buchanan who was evidently enjoying the spectacle.

As the dark-haired and dark-eyed Susie strutted across the stage with a powerful show of confidence aided by her undoubted beauty and grace, Mrs Buchanan gave her full support, applauding and cheering as Susie clearly scored points with her charm, her intelligent answers and her beguiling way of smiling at each judge as if he or she was the only person in the world. When all the girls had performed their necessary ritual, the judges declared they would retire to consider their verdict, a difficult task which was expected to take some thirty or forty minutes; meanwhile, the girls could get dressed in their day clothes and during the wait for the result, refreshments would be served by the WI.

It was an agonizing wait for everyone, especially the girls and their families, but I was impressed by the good-natured rapport between everyone, contestants and spectators alike. The competitors were friendly with each other too and so were their parents, and I saw Walter shyly approach Mrs Buchanan and wish her all the best for Susie's success. It was while observing this passing show that Arthur Drake, the local butcher, turned up at my side and spoke to me.

'You're watching Walter at work I bet,' he grinned mischievously, clearly recognizing my interest.

'At work?' I was puzzled by his phrase.

'Working on Jessie Buchanan,' he smiled. 'Trying his best to get her interested in him. Why do you think he made such a fuss to get this competition under way?'

'I've no idea,' I shrugged. 'I thought he proposed it as some kind of benefit for the village.'

'Aye, it is, but it's of benefit to Walter as well, or it will be if young Susie wins.'

'I don't follow your logic, Arthur,' I had to admit.

'Well, I've known Walter a long time, we're good pals, always have been, but he's a bit deep, never says much but thinks a lot. He's a very straight sort of a chap but those who know him well, like me, reckon he's taken a shine to Mrs Buchanan.'

'That doesn't surprise me,' I said. 'Two lonely people with similar interests, each losing a partner and living fairly close to each other. I'd say it makes sense for them to do things together sometimes, even if there is no romance.'

'Walter's not the romantic type, Nick, that's his problem. He fancies Mrs Buchanan like mad though, and he'd love to romance her, but he'll never let her know how he feels.'

'Well, he's just wished her all the best for Susie, I saw him,' I said. 'And it was Walter who proposed this contest, you know. He's bound to be interested in the outcome and he'll want to know whether or not it's been a success.'

'Aye, but why did he suggest it in the first place, Nick? Just you think about that.'

'Well, he is a parish councillor and I thought he wanted something special for Aidensfield, an event which would put the village on the map.'

'Or an event which would put him in favour with Mrs Buchanan?' Arthur looked at me with a glint in his eye. 'I think we all know Susie will win; she was the best by far up on that stage. And that's just what Walter wants. And remember, everybody in Aidensfield knows the beauty contest was Walter's idea.'

'Yes, the news has spread fairly widely,' I agreed.

'And Mrs Ramsbottom helped, she did a good job letting us all know how decadent he is!'

'Arthur, you're still talking in riddles. How does Arthur hope to impress Mrs Buchanan by organizing a beauty contest for the pretty young things of this village?'

'By not being a judge, Nick.'

'Go on, I need more explanation, Arthur. I know he'd turned down the offer of being one of the judges—that did surprise me, I must admit, as the whole thing was his idea. I thought he'd have loved to be a judge.'

'Not him. He didn't want to be a judge in case he had to decide Susie wasn't the winner, or that she was the winner.'

'Now you're even more baffling!' I said, waiting for his explanation of this conundrum.

'Right, Nick. Walter's been a judge for years and years, livestock, domestic pets, vegetables, fruit, flowers, local crafts even. You name it and Walter's been a judge of it, mainly in local shows but sometimes further afield such as Stokesley Show, Egton Show and once at the Great Yorkshire. He takes his duties very seriously, Nick, and he would always be totally impartial. No friend of Walter's would, or should, expect any favours. In fact, he might even give second place to a first winner if it happened to be a friend; he wouldn't want to be accused of bias in favour of a friend. That's how strict he is with himself.'

'Go on,' I invited.

'Well, can't you see what he's done?' Arthur sounded puzzled by my stupidity.

'No, I can't. What's he done?'

'Well, Nick, cast your mind back to Aidensfield Show three years ago, when Walter was a judge . . . it was the first show after Tim Buchanan had died. Tim always won in the horticultural classes, firsts in most cases, with Walter as judge. And so he should, he produced the best stuff.'

'So?'

'After he died, Jessie showed her produce in various classes, first with stuff grown by her husband, and later with stuff she grew herself. But whenever Walter was a judge, she never got a first—and he was a judge at most of the shows in Aidensfield and district. She was so keen to win because it would help put her market garden in the spotlight, all good for future business, but Walter marked them all down, whether it was her taties or carrots or tomatoes or cabbages, flowers too. It didn't matter what it was or how good it was, he allus gave her seconds and thirds, or sometimes just a Highly Commended. Never a first prize.'

'Perhaps there was a reason, Arthur? Like they only deserved seconds and thirds?'

'I'm sure some did, but most of her stuff was top rate, it should have won.'

'So why did Walter never award her a first prize? It seems wrong to me that he would mark her down when she deserved to win.'

'He thought he was being biased in her favour if he awarded her firsts,' smiled Arthur. 'And being a scrupulously fair judge he could never bear to think he was giving her a first just because he had such strong feelings for her. It was all in his head, you see. He reckoned that if he gave her first prize time and time again, he'd be criticized because he was favouring her, because he fancied her, to put it simply. And folks knew he did anyway. But he was involved in a dilemma of his own making. To be honest, it was all in his mind, it still is, Nick. Folks wouldn't have minded her winning time and time again if she deserved it, which she did.'

'So the outcome was that the more he fancied her or longed for her, the more he was likely to upset her by failing to award her the prizes she had earned. It's an odd way to behave, Arthur.'

'It is, but that's how Walter's mind has been working all this time. Not wanting to show his feelings for her by giving her firsts, not letting outsiders know how he was wanting to show his passion for her, and not opening himself up to criticism from others because of awarding the love of his life first prizes . . .'

'Right.' I could now see how the self-imposed dilemma had affected poor old Walter. 'So, Arthur, how does all this fit in with his idea of staging a beauty contest?'

'Well, Jessie Buchanan has produced a very beautiful and intelligent daughter, one who deserves first prize, in Walter's estimation.'

'Another type of produce, eh?' I laughed.

'Right. And so Walter wondered if she might one day win a prize—Susie I mean—and so I suggested he should arrange a beauty contest.'

'*You* suggested it?'

'Aye, Nick. I know Walter very well you see, and I knew what was going through his mind, how he was torturing himself, so I told him to persuade the parish council to stage a beauty contest to give Susie and her mum a fair chance at winning, but I also told him to be sure he was not appointed one of the judges.'

'You crafty old schemer! So if Susie wins, she'll bring praise and publicity to Aidensfield, and also to her mum's market garden?'

'Aye,' nodded Arthur. 'Jessie deserves some success, you know.'

'And Walter agreed?'

'He did; he said he would put the idea to the parish council and look what's happened! A lovely occasion, Nick, with everyone happy except Mrs Ramsbottom, and there's Walter doing his best to have a quiet word with Jessie Buchanan, see? Over there near the stage. They're chatting like old pals—oh, and he told me he's going to retire from judging at shows. He wants to be free from upsetting folks by not giving them first prize.'

'So whatever happens here today, Walter is a free man?'

'He is, and I'm really pleased for him. And he does seem to be hitting it off with Jessie, doesn't he?'

I looked across at the couple; they were chatting and laughing like old friends and I felt Arthur had really done a huge service to his old friend. And then the announcement came that the judges had reached a decision and would announce it within five minutes.

The girls had to return to the stage in their ordinary day clothes and the audience was asked to return to their seats.

Susie Buchanan was declared the winner. The judges said their decision was unanimous and she was awarded the

£100 first prize, a sash bearing the title Miss Aidensfield and a trip to London for herself and her mother. And as I watched the celebrations, I saw Mrs Buchanan throw her arms around Walter and plant a huge kiss on his lips and she said, 'Oh, thank you, Walter, for making all this possible . . .'

Whether Mrs Buchanan ever felt she was being discriminated against in her desire to win trophies for her produce, I shall never know, but when she went off to London with Susie she asked Walter to care for her market garden. And he accepted with lots of blushing and heartbeating; anyone would have thought he'd won a fortune on the football pools.

Susie also won the Miss Heather Belle contest later in the year and afterwards Walter spent a lot of time helping in the market garden, not only when Jessie was away. Some of the Buchanan-grown produce won first prizes at various shows the following year too, including the Great Yorkshire, but whether that was due to Walter's influence or Jessie's skill was never revealed.

Those of us who knew the story behind this blossoming romance then waited for Walter to pop the question. It would be a long wait, we reckoned. If we truly wanted that to happen, most of us felt someone should have a word with Arthur, as we thought he might need a gentle nudge of some kind. Someone might find a way of persuading Walter to be brave—but we wouldn't rush things too much.

* * *

It was not uncommon in villages and farmsteads upon the moors around my home to find men of all ages who had never married. There used to be a belief that such bachelors were sexually inadequate or homosexual, but in most of the moorland cases, this was far from true. These bachelors were hard-working, tough men with uncomplicated sexual appetites and desires but whose way of life and work had never brought them into contact with available young women. They buried themselves in their work as the years whizzed past at an astonishing rate and suddenly discovered they were too old to worry about their station in life, or now lacked any interest in pursuing desirable damsels, let alone the damsel of their youthful dreams. Most of these men were extremely lonely but life had presented them with a tough deal from which, in most cases, there was no escape. They worked seven days a week for 365 days a year, usually from dawn until dusk, their only relaxation being the deep sleep of the busy person. Many were too weary even to visit the pub.

Such a man was Ernie Jackson of Hollin Edge Farm high on the moors above Gelderslack. Ernie's parents owned the farm, each of them working day and night to scratch a meagre living from the rugged landscape. They kept sheep, pigs and poultry and managed to survive, chiefly because the farm had been handed down through generations of Jacksons. There was no mortgage on the property and it was not rented from a local estate like so many similar premises but in spite of that, the eternal shortage of money meant it had become rather run-down and in need of modernization.

There was no electricity at the farm in the 1960s and no running water. Things like electric cookers, cleaners, lights, and radio or television were unknown in the Jackson household; the house was heated by a turf fire, lighting was by oil lamps, and the toilet was a crude affair outside which could be cleaned periodically by diverting a moorland stream through it. A man-made minor dam had been effected to facilitate this; a stout door could be lifted to let the water flow along a stone channel to do nature's vital task. One did not ask where the effluent terminated. This was primitive Yorkshire but it was the way Ernie's father, grandfather and great-grandfather, and all the Jackson men before him, had been reared. None had thought to question, criticize or change his basic way of life.

If one should ask where these men of former times had found their womenfolk, the answer was that many farms, probably until the outbreak of World War II, employed hired hands, male or female, most of whom lived in. Many of these were young girls—milkmaids, servant girls, cowgirls and such—and they found romance among the heather. It was surprising how many of them married the sons of the household in which they found employment. This arrangement hardly changed their lifetime's commitment to hard work and poverty, but it provided a roof over their head while offering some welcome security.

There was no such luck for Ernie. His mother had been a maid on a large spread nearby; she had met Ernie's father and married him, but money had always been short and Ernie's father had not been able to afford to pay staff. Ernie was their work-force.

He had started work on the farm even as a primary-school boy, cleaning out the hens, collecting eggs, helping at haytime and potato picking, coping with the milking, lambing and sheep clipping even before reaching the age of ten. He did all this, day in, day out, without a holiday save for the occasional day trip with his school to Scarborough at Whitsuntide. He worked like this, without complaint, because he knew no other way of life and, of course, he also knew that one day he would inherit the family farm. He would never be a farm labourer—he was a yeoman farmer. That's how the system worked—farms were handed down to the eldest son, and as Ernie was an only child, it was a foregone conclusion that he would inherit the farm when his parents died. They would never retire, they could not afford to, neither would they go to live in an old folks' home or council bungalow; they would live at the farm until the very end and so it happened. Ma and Pa Jackson died within weeks of one another, leaving Ernie to run the farm entirely on his own. He was now a yeoman farmer with a spread of his very own, a real bachelor of the moors.

In spite of their poverty, both Ma and Pa had put small amounts of money aside for the proverbial rainy day. Not trusting banks, however, they had diligently stuffed their spare cash into milk churns in the larder; at the end of each week, they totted up their accounts and all the profit, or the week's unspent housekeeping money was 'put by' as they called it. It was 'put by' before it could be spent and it was never used, always there in case of real emergency. Thus a useful cache of money had accumulated over more than forty years. After his parents' death, Ernie found it and realized he could do something useful with it.

No one was quite sure how much this treasure trove was, but it was enough for Ernie to have electricity and water installed in the remote farm. Suddenly, he found himself using machines to milk the cows, electric shears to clip sheep, and electric lights and power in the house. He fitted a water-operated indoor toilet along with a bathroom and hot water in his taps, and then he resurfaced the old track down to his farm until it was a smooth carriageway.

Finally he bought himself a car which was infinitely more suitable than the tractor for some of his new activities; true, it was a second-hand and fairly ancient Humber Super Snipe, but it was a splendid vehicle in superb condition and big enough to accommodate his two sheep dogs or even a sheep or two if necessary. Ernie's life had changed for the better and he began to come down into Aidensfield for essentials at the shop, or even drive into Eltering to the cattle mart—once, he even bought himself a pair of new corduroy trousers and a jacket, and then, once a week on a Saturday night, he would come to the pub for a couple of pints and a bar snack. Soon, he was joining other men in the bar, enjoying a game of dominoes or darts and finding himself discussing the trials and tribulations of Middlesbrough football club or the Yorkshire cricket team.

But one facet of Ernie's life did not change: he didn't find himself a girlfriend. The truth was, of course, he didn't seek one. As a confirmed bachelor in his late thirties, it had never occurred to him that a woman might share his life or would even want to, and his resistance to this most basic of ideas became one of the chief talking points whenever he was in the pub among friends.

'What thoo needs, awd Ernie lad, is a good warm woman to go home to on a cawd neet,' I heard one of his pals exclaim while I was enjoying a relaxed evening in the bar. 'It's tahmn thoo settled doon wiv a wife and mebbe even started breeding, thoo'll 'ave to leave t'farm ti somebody when thoo dees. It'll be worth a few thousand quid, thoo knaws, thoo can't let this government get their hands on it. So git thisen a good woman, start breeding and give thissen summat ti work for.'

Faced with teasing of this kind at frequent intervals, Ernie would merely blush and shake his head, sometimes saying 'No woman would have me. What have Ah got ti offer?' or 'Ah'm as 'appy as Ah can be, Ah do what Ah want when Ah want and how Ah want,' or 'They tell me women cost a lot ti keep, more than a new car, they reckon, allus wanting new clothes and takking off ti t'shops, and Ah'm not sure Ah could afford a family anyroad.'

The banter was always good natured and Ernie appeared to enjoy it, invariably finding some reason why he did not want to be bothered with women and it was clear that he was the epitome of a confirmed bachelor. One Saturday night, however, I popped into the pub with Mary, my wife; we had decided to enjoy a brief night out, thanks to Mrs Quarry, our baby-sitter, and our intention was to have a bar snack. Tucked into one corner close to the bar counter was Ernie with three of his pals. They were sitting at a table playing fives and threes, a popular variety of the game of dominoes, and there was the usual happy banter between them.

As we enjoyed the atmosphere and the food, I noted Edwin Lambert, a thick-set and well-to-do farmer from Maddleskirk.

He walked past Mary and me, plonked an empty pint glass on the counter and said to the men at Ernie's table and to the landlord, 'Well, it's an early night for me. Crack of dawn start tomorrow; me and our Vera are off to Spain. See you chaps in ten days' time.'

'Spain?' somebody called out to him. 'What are you going t' Spain for?'

'I thought I might take in a bullfight, but from what I've seen of them Spanish bulls, my awd Charolais, Chubby, would make a better job of seeing off them matadors, or whatever they're called.'

'Bullfighting!' snorted one of Ernie's pals. 'You're not going bullfighting. You're going to see all those lovely Spanish *señoritas* . . . I'd better have a word with your wife, tell her to keep you on a tight rein!'

'Well, I can't see I need one, but I did think I might find one for Ernie. How do you fancy that, Ernie? A nice raven-haired Spanish *señorita* to come and wave her castanets at you? Shall I have words with one or two when I'm over there?' chuckled Edwin. 'I'd say you'd be in big demand—a good-looking chap like you with a big house and acres of land and a big car! I might just pass the word around . . .'

Ernie merely grinned at the taunt and concentrated on trying to produce a total of fifteen from his hand of dominoes and so Edwin departed, chuckling to himself as the rest of us settled down to the remainder of the evening. I gave no further thought to Edwin's minor teasing nor of Ernie's marital prospects. Then things changed. Several months later, I was manning the desk in Ashfordly police office when the door opened.

In walked a smartly dressed but rather plump-looking foreign woman of about thirty-five with black hair, black eyes and a very pretty face bearing a confident smile. Such arrivals were a fairly regular feature of most police stations because, at that time, even more than twenty years after the war, England was still recovering from the effects of World War II and foreigners, whom we termed 'aliens' were subject to a range of restrictions if they came to the UK. One of the pieces of legislation was the Aliens Order of 1953 and, subject to other controls by the Minister of Labour or the immigration authorities, the basic rule was that any alien coming to the UK under restrictions on the length of their stay had to register with the police.

The alien had to produce his or her passport or other document of identity to the police and so we, even the lowest rank of police constable, could find ourselves processing such arrivals so that the incoming foreigner could be issued with a document known as an Aliens Registration Certificate. This might include certain conditions about their employment or place of residence and the certificates had to be carried at all times during their stay in this country and produced to the police or immigration officials on demand. This lady, I guessed, had come to find employment.

'*Buenos dias,*' she smiled, as she reached the counter and placed her passport upon it.

'*Buenos dias,*' I returned, adding, '*Habla ingles?*'

'A leetle,' she smiled at me. 'A very leetle,'

'*No hablo mucho español,*' I admitted.

And so we began our conversation in her 'leetle' English and my extremely 'leetle' Spanish. From her documents, I saw she had come to England to find work and the immigration authorities had imposed an initial six-month limit upon her stay. I saw no flaws in her documents and managed to make it known to her that her ARC (Alien's Registration Certificate) would cost five shillings. When the formalities were complete, she then produced a piece of paper bearing a name and address, and asked if I could direct her to it. I was somewhat surprised to see the name was Ernie Jackson and the address was his farm at Gelderslack.

It was not my business to question her as to how she had come to have Ernie's name and address, but I suspected it was somehow connected with Edwin Lambert's recent trip to Spain.

'Is Mr Jackson expecting you?' I asked.

'No, eet ees surprise, very big surprise,' she beamed, her eyes wide with anticipation.

As it was clear Ernie was not expecting to collect her, I told her about a bus service which carried her to the lane end of his farm and advised her to ask the driver to let her know when she had reached it; upon disembarking, there would be a walk of almost half a mile.

'No problem,' she beamed with the calm of a continental lady.

At that stage, I think I was the only person, apart from Ernie himself, to know about the arrival of the Spanish *señorita* and over the next few days, I heard or saw nothing more of her.

But Ernie stunned both his friends and the entire village because she arrived at the pub with him the following Saturday night, and she looked radiant, stunning and completely contented. He had smartened up too, and for the first time in years, looked extremely cheerful. All those previous taunts of Ernie's love-life, or lack of it, now turned to undisguised admiration as Maria charmed everyone. She became the centre of attention while Ernie said nowt about it. His happy smile said everything.

It was no surprise therefore, when, a few months later, Ernie announced he was going to get married to Maria; he was even thinking of selling up and going to live in Spain to live on the proceeds.

I think a lot of people wondered why Edwin Lambert was invited to be the best man.

CHAPTER 5

When I was a growing lad, many of my contemporaries wanted to be airline pilots, engine drivers or firemen when they grew up. Others were content to join the family business or seek a military career; yet others were happy to learn trades and so become bricklayers, plumbers, carpenters or electricians. Some, however, had ambitions to join the police service in the hope of becoming famous detectives. Girls adopted a similar attitude. Some thought the police would make a good and interesting career of benefit to society in general although most saw themselves as ministering angels in our hospitals, or air hostesses in smart uniforms. Lots opted for secretarial skills and some even dreamt of being famous actresses and film stars.

I am sure many determined youngsters managed to fulfil their career ambitions, but usually their fantasies were never achieved. It was one of those oddities of nature that those who most desperately wanted to be police officers or famous detectives—men or women—were often unsuitable or unqualified to join the force, and the same logic applied to the other desirable professions. So many dreams often remained unfulfilled. When it came to wanting a career in the police, therefore, there were many unhappy rejects, many being due to nothing more than failing to reach the minimum height. It was often argued that small people could become very good detectives but the authorities wanted their police officers to be taller than average—at least six feet in some cases. On many occasions when a person was rejected, a suitable alternative job would present itself and many a would-be copper succeeded in a totally different career.

Some, however, refused to accept rejection. When we discovered that a fake policemen was stopping and fining motorists on the roads around Ashfordly, it took a while for us to realize it might be someone whose constabulary ambitions had been thwarted. Our first instinct was that the culprit was someone determined to wreak revenge upon motorists for reasons we could not determine, or else someone who had found a ready means of earning some extra tax-free cash. There was no way we could estimate how many drivers had been stopped by this man nor did we know how long he had been operating. Furthermore, he selected a different stretch of road for each of his swoops; the timing of his offences varied slightly too.

His *modus operandi* made it extremely difficult either to trace him or predict his next move, although his technique was rather simple. Dressed in what looked like a police uniform, he would halt a driver who had committed some minor traffic offence, such as exceeding the speed limit, obstructing the highway, a breach of the parking regulations, driving without lights, crossing a double white line, failing to give a proper signal when turning left or right or failing to stop at a HALT sign. He would lecture those motorists on their poor standard of driving and then raise the subject of a penalty suitable for their misdemeanours. He warned them they faced the risk of going to court with the possibility of a stiff sentence, and of course, endorsement of their driving licence. To obviate that risk, he then explained, they could pay an on-the-spot penalty and that would be the end of the matter. It was a simple solution and he assured them there would be no further action.

The fines he levied were usually £2 or £3, quite small by some standards, and if his 'customer' agreed to that course of action he would issue what looked like a genuine receipt. Few people mentioned this experience to others, especially not to police officers, because they were relieved to be treated with such leniency. Furthermore, they were very pleased at not having to attend court and most relieved not to suffer an endorsement on their driving licence. And, it seemed, they had in fact committed the offence for which they had been fined and so they found no just cause for complaint. The experience would also serve as a reminder that they should constantly strive to improve their driving standards—as our hero boldly suggested to each of his 'customers'.

Catching him in the act of impersonating a police officer was far from easy. It was likely that if we arranged uniformed officers or marked cars to patrol the roads deliberately to catch him, he would notice them and be deterred from his activities. If that happened, he would never be caught. Stealth, based on the limited intelligence we had received, seemed the only solution.

We first learned of his activities by chance because he made the mistake of 'fining' the wife of a genuine serving policeman. She was Clare Milburn, the wife of PC Derek Milburn, one of the constables stationed at Brantsford. That was a small market town which had recently been amalgamated with Ashfordly section—the same sergeant supervised both Brantsford and Ashfordly Sections. Clare, in her mid-thirties, had been driving through Ashfordly just before 5.30 p.m. one Wednesday afternoon when she had stopped to post some letters.

She worked as a secretary in a local estate office and had been asked to drop the day's mail into the letter box on her way home. It was one of her regular tasks. On this occasion, however, because there was also a parcel to post along with an unusually large number of letters, and because she was in a hurry to get home to collect her two children from a friend's house, she parked as close as possible to the post office. In fact, she parked right outside the main door. That happened to be a 'No Parking' area, but as she expected to be no longer than a few seconds, she took the risk.

Unfortunately, there was a queue at the counter and her mission took longer than expected. When she came out, a policeman was inspecting her car and noting its registration number. She approached him in something of a fluster whereupon he gave her a polite telling-off and imposed a spot fine of £2. He gave her a receipt and she hurried home in the knowledge she could have suffered the indignity of being summoned to attend court with the risk of a greater and more public penalty. In spite of her tenseness during those few moments, she felt there was something not quite right about the policeman—his general demeanour did not seem true, in her opinion, neither did she know him. She thought he must be new to the job, an inexperienced raw recruit; he was very young; and so, with those few very slight concerns, she tried to forget the incident. Most certainly, she did not mention it to Derek—it wasn't the sort of thing one mentions to one's policeman husband!

A day or two later it was Derek's day off and he used the car to go fishing. He then found the receipt for £2 in the glove compartment. Clare had pushed it there during her rush to get home and had forgotten about it, but it puzzled Derek. It was printed in black with the words POLICE TRAFFIC LAW ENFORCEMENT on the top, and lines below bearing in handwritten words the note 'Fine for causing obstruction in No Parking area—£2' followed by a signature which was indecipherable. It was followed by the word 'Constable'.

Derek smelt a rat. For one thing, there were no such forms in use within the Force, it did not bear the Force's name and it looked very amateurish. In his view, it looked as if it had been produced on a home printing set and then photocopied. The real clue, however, was that the fixed penalty procedure, introduced as recently as 1967 by the Road Traffic Regulation Act of that year, had generated its own special form. This allowed offenders to test the case in court if they wished. If not, he or she could opt to pay the prescribed fixed penalty—which was never an on-the-spot fine. The genuine form was quite comprehensive and presented the alternatives in a manner prescribed by law, as well as detailing the offence and the statute which had been infringed.

Indeed, there were no 'on-the-spot' fines of any kind at that time and the new fixed penalties could not be imposed on the spot. If fixed penalty notices were served, either by a police officer or one of the recently introduced traffic wardens, the offender had twenty-one days in which to either pay the fine or volunteer to attend court to fight the case. No one had to pay immediately.

Derek spoke to his wife who initially thought he was angry because she had been fined and so she was somewhat reticent about the matter, but when she realized she had been the victim of some kind of confidence trick, she told him the whole story. Being a good policeman with a sound interviewing technique, he managed to elicit a good deal of information from Clare and then spoke to Sergeant Craddock. This incident did not occur during my spell as acting sergeant, by the way, and Craddock listened carefully, then decided to summon us to a conference in his office.

'This is the situation,' he explained. 'A fake constable is apparently operating in this area and levying on-the-spot fines to motorists. We do not know the extent of his activities, nor do we know how long he has been operating or how many victims he has fined. He is thought to be in his twenties with a slim build and perhaps not tall enough to be a genuine officer. He has dark hair which, for the area showing beneath his cap, was cut short but he has no other identifying features on his face. No moustache, no moles, and we don't know the colour of his eyes. He was wearing a police uniform, or what appeared to be a police uniform; it was good enough to fool Clare Milburn although she did sense it was not quite correct, or that his demeanour was not quite correct. She thought he was about her height which is five feet eight inches, not tall enough to join our Force. That could explain why she sensed that things weren't quite right and on reflection, she thought he looked like a constable on the stage rather than a real one. In her moments of anxiety, she put it down to his inexperience or youthfulness.'

He went on to say that Clare had described his uniform as being navy-blue serge trousers, black boots, a police tunic with silver buttons, a blue shirt and black tie, and a peaked cap with a badge at the front.

Craddock told us he had alerted Divisional Headquarters, Sub-Division and the Road Traffic Division, and he had asked them, and was asking us, to try and ascertain if the counterfeit copper had tricked anyone else. He also added that consideration had been given to highlighting his activities in the press but this had been rejected, temporarily at least, because such publicity might cause him to go to ground in which case he might never be apprehended—and he could then start all over again elsewhere. Craddock did stress, however, that no one knew whether Clare was his only victim although she did say he had a thick wad of his 'receipts' and seemed quite practised in the way he delivered his reprimand and issued his fine. She felt he had done this sort of thing many times before.

'So where has he obtained his uniform?' Craddock put to us. 'Is it one he has mocked up from spare pieces, or is it a complete uniform? Has he a relation in the Force, or one who was a former police officer who has retained some of his uniform? Or is it a stage uniform? He may be guilty of offences under the Police Act of 1964—impersonating a police officer, wearing a uniform calculated to deceive others, or of course, being in unlawful possession of items of police uniform. All those offences carry heavy fines, and he has also obtained cash by deception. So there we are, gentlemen, someone is falsely parading as a policeman—he shouldn't take much finding, should he?'

Craddock instructed us to be cautious in the way we dealt with this enquiry because we did not want to frighten off our quarry. We wanted to trap him, to catch him in the act and bring him before the court where the public would learn of his antics and be warned of others who might emulate him. The sergeant asked us to make discreet enquiries on our beats and generate some gossip in an effort to determine whether there had been other instances of this kind; he wanted us to try and establish an identifiable pattern to his behaviour and he asked us to try and locate the source of his illicit uniform.

Thanks to the diligence of my colleagues in Ashfordly, Brantsford, Eltering and district, in asking around pubs, clubs and places of public resort, news of our interest in the spot-fine constable spread rapidly. People began to talk about it and very soon further instances of his activities began to emerge. Between them, those officers discovered fifteen other occasions where people had been stopped, warned about their driving standards and 'fined' £2 or £3 by a young policeman. One or two of the cases were passed to us at third hand with the victims' names being unknown, but in some cases it had been possible to trace the victims and obtain their stories, albeit with an assurance they would not be prosecuted by us for their 'offences'! In fact, of course, we had no evidence of their wrongdoing. All had been happy to pay the fines rather than risk a court appearance, but most said they'd rather pay a genuine penalty than a fictitious one! But in assessing these cases, some interesting facts emerged. One was that the fake constable did not appear to make use of a vehicle of any kind.

Even though one or two of his victims had been 'fined' for speeding in built-up areas, they had not been followed by a police vehicle. The pseudo-constable had appeared in the road ahead to flag down the drivers concerned, make his accusations and collect the fines. Although he had no evidence of actual speeding, other than his opinion they had been going too fast in a built-up area, most of the victims agreed they had exceeded the speed limit just as others agreed they had committed minor traffic offences. One had jumped the traffic lights at red only to find the constable waiting for him; others had been parked in restricted areas to achieve some urgent purpose; one had had a broken headlight on his car and another had crossed the double white lines on a corner. And in all instances, our fictitious constable had been able to halt their cars, give a lecture on road craft and then collect his fine. But if we had managed to trace these people in such a short time, how many more unknown victims were there? Apart from his criminal activities, there was a strong chance this character was making a very useful tax-free income.

After a fortnight of failing to catch him, but with quite a useful amount of information already to hand from all over the sub-division, it was decided we should all pool our growing file of information. A larger conference would be held in Eltering Court House which adjoined Eltering Police Station and it would comprise officers from the whole of the sub-division, almost forty in all. It would be hosted by Inspector Tom Ashton of the Eltering Area Traffic Department who had been collating the enquiries. The inspector had done some sound work and had personally re-interviewed several of the victims in his effort to gather supportive facts.

He outlined the case for those less familiar with events and then went on to the finer points.

'First,' he said, 'his description. After talking to several witnesses, I believe he is in his early twenties, about five feet eight inches tall, slim build with dark hair cut short, good teeth and grey eyes. He is well spoken with no discernible accent and appears to have a knowledge of traffic law—but he could get that from a book in the library or even the Highway Code. He is very clean, his boots are highly polished, his trousers are pressed and the peak of his cap is polished too. One alert witness thought his cap badge was old-fashioned, though, he said it bore the King's crown, not the Queen's but interestingly enough in spite of the general view that he was smart, several thought his uniform looked ill-fitting. Although it was clean and tidy—which some might interpret as smart— his jacket looked baggy, his trousers were fractionally too long and his cap came down over his ears but not low enough to hide his hairline. I have spoken to Clare Milburn because her first impression was that he did not look the part. His height was one factor and it seems now, on reflection, she thinks he did not wear a whistle chain, nor did his jacket have numerals on the shoulders. I have checked this with other witnesses and some agree with that. This raises the question whether the jacket is a real police uniform or just a navy tunic with silver-coloured buttons? Dark trousers, blue shirts, black ties and black boots can be obtained from almost anywhere, and navy-blue peaked caps aren't difficult to come by, nor are chromium-plated cap badges. It means he might not be wearing an actual police uniform, but something cobbled together to give that general appearance.'

A member of his audience now put up his hand and said, 'Sir, I've been to all the theatrical suppliers, amateur theatre groups and second-hand shops in this area, but I've not found anyone who has either lost or supplied a police-style uniform. They're all helping by keeping their ears and eyes open.'

'Thanks, we need to find other places where he might have obtained the clothes which make up his uniform, either in parts or as a whole. That's an ongoing task for all of you. Now, there is another valuable point to consider. The timing of his offences. Although one of them occurred at 9.30 a.m., on a Monday, all the others have been between 4 p.m. and 6 p.m. on weekdays. That might be significant.'

He paused to let us digest that piece of information, then went on, 'Another factor, so it would appear, is that he manages to target victims who are rushing somewhere—rushing to pick up the children from school or child carers, rushing home from work, rushing back to the office before knocking-off time . . . of the fifteen cases we know about, seven were young women rushing to collect children from school, three were men dashing to meetings—one was his 9.30 a.m. catch—and the others were people leaving work and either going straight home or doing some minor task on the way. People often rush home from work and he seems to know who they are. In every case, they were only too pleased to pay their fine and continue their journey. So how does he select such people? And how significant is the timing of his offences?'

Again the inspector paused to let us ponder those questions before continuing with, 'If he has a job, it is one which allows him freedom at those times. A shift-worker perhaps? Someone on permanent nights? In a factory? On the railways?'

There were quite a number of nearby places of employment which used shift-workers, including hospitals, fire stations, the railways, the post office, a meat factory and distant places like ICI and various works on Teesside or in West Yorkshire. It occurred to me that a railway uniform could be made to look like a policeman's, as could a postman's. All wore navy-blue peaked caps—our policemen did not wear helmets at that time.

Inspector Ashton continued, 'Being a shift-worker might explain those times, but if he has no job, why select that particular time to act? Is it because he knows people rush home from work and are prone to take risks when driving under those conditions, or is it because that is the only time he is free to indulge in his odd spare-time occupation? I might add that we have asked his victims whether they have angered anyone of this description in any way, whether he is getting his revenge for some past incident but this does not appear to be his motive. His only motive, so it would seem, is that he likes to impose his own penalties on drivers who break the law and we have found no common link between his victims—other than him, of course. Now, another aspect of his behaviour has puzzled us—how does he manage to parade in public places in a police uniform without any of the regular officers noticing him? Or without a member of the public growing suspicious? And how does he travel from place to place? He has operated in small communities some distance from one another—Ashfordly, Eltering and Brantsford in fact, all market towns with narrow streets, lots of side alleys, shops and so forth.'

Ashton paused again, allowing us to mull over his words.

'One very good witness recalled a brown canvas hold-all in an alley just where he pulled up her car. She thought it was an odd place for a hold-all to be left and there was no one with it. Did it belong to chummy? Does he wear an overcoat over his uniform while travelling to his scenes or even while waiting for his prey to come along, or does he use one to conceal himself from the real police, and does he carry his cap in the hold-all? Once he has selected his scene, does he then hide his coat in the hold-all while he is carrying out his self-imposed law enforcement? These are just thoughts, we have no real evidence to support them, but if you think along these lines, you might produce an answer or two. And you might catch chummy. He must be caught.'

'It sounds as if he's doing a good job on our behalf!' laughed one of the audience. 'All those law-breakers caught and punished! Maybe we could learn something from him?'

'Well, it's significant that none of his victims has lodged an official complaint and clearly, he's dedicated to his task. And that reminds me! We haven't established his motive for doing this,' added Ashton. 'If you can determine that, it might lead you to him. So, that's all I can offer at the moment. It's down to you now, so return to your beats, ask around and try to work out who fits this rather sketchy pro-file of an avenging knight in shining black boots.'

We left the conference with a determination to trace this man but we knew his crimes weren't like others.

In most other cases when someone became the victim, they reported it to the police and in that way we became aware of the problem; in this case, none of the victims had reported their experience to the real police, and, we knew, future victims would probably not do so either. We would have to spread the word among the public and listen to gos-sip! We had to find reliable witnesses, however, and so we must encourage people to chatter about him—and we had to tap into that chatter if we were to learn more about his behaviour.

As I drove back to Aidensfield I began to wonder about his motive. As Inspector Ashton had admitted, we had no idea why he was perpetrating these acts, but as I thought about the case, three factors dawned upon me: one was his age. All the witnesses said he was a young man, some suggesting he was in his twenties or even his early twenties. The second factor was his uniform. Although clean, witnesses said it was ill-fitting and too large for him, and the third factor was his height. Five feet eight inches or so, according to several reliable witnesses. That was too small to join the North Riding Constabulary. Its minimum height requirement for men was five feet ten inches, although the London Metropolitan Police would accept men of five feet eight inches; the provincial forces called them metronomes!

By the time I returned to Aidensfield, I was wondering whether our man was someone who had been rejected by the police service. The age was right—we recruited men between the ages of eighteen and thirty. Another consideration was that a man of five foot eight inches might find difficulty being accepted by any of the provincial police forces; certainly he could not become a constable in my force.

His educational abilities were another factor as was his physical condition, all of which meant a candidate could be rejected for several reasons.

I returned to the little office at the side of my police house and rang a colleague in the recruiting department of my own Force. In addition to handling applications for the local Force, they were sometimes asked to assist in processing applicants for elsewhere.

'Recruiting,' answered a male voice. 'Sergeant Collins speaking.'

'Hello, Sergeant,' I responded, giving my name.

'Now young Rhea,' he replied, remembering me because he had recruited me several years earlier. 'What can I do for you?'

I told him as much as I knew about the fake policeman and then asked, 'The reason I'm ringing is that I wonder if anyone of that description had applied to join the Force recently, and been rejected. It could be someone local to the Ashfordly, Brantsford, Eltering area.'

Sergeant Collins possessed an encyclopaedic knowledge of recruits old and new and in recent years, there had not been a particularly heavy list of applicants—other professions offered high salaries without the need to work shifts and they selected their recruits from the same pool of young men. With somewhat fewer candidates to consider, Collins could recall details of each person who had applied to join our Force.

'It sounds like young Groves to me,' he said. 'Michael Groves. Do you know him?'

'Sorry, Sergeant, no I don't.'

'His parents have a smart hotel in your part of the world, Ghylldale Hall. It used to be a country house. They bought it ten years ago when it was nearly derelict, and turned it into a very smart hotel. It's popular with shooting parties and fishermen, that sort of place. Michael works for them, he's the barman among other things, but he felt he wanted something better and opted for a police career. He applied a few months ago, Nick, but we had to turn him down. He was bright enough but he was a couple of inches too small and he had been injured in a car accident as a child, he's not an invalid, but is slightly deformed as a result. One of his shoulders is out of alignment, just a little . . . in all honesty, we couldn't accept him.'

I thought that could explain the baggy appearance of the tunic worn by our suspect or even his too-long trousers. Sergeant Collins produced another three names from the locality, one of whom had been accepted by Middlesbrough Borough Police after being rejected by our own force due to his height (5' 9") while the other two had been accepted by our own Force. One or two other applicants had written to ask for details of a police career but had not followed up their initial approach but neither was from the locality in which I was interested.

Sergeant Collins thought Michael Groves appeared to be a very intense young man who was acutely disappointed at his rejection even though the sergeant suggested he might apply to the London Metropolitan Police or one of the other constabulary services such as British Transport Police, the various ports or dock police, the parks police or some other specialist police service.

There were many such forces in addition to the county, city and borough constabularies of the time. I thanked Sergeant Collins for his help and was now faced with finding out more about Michael Groves. His name would not appear in criminal records because that would have been checked upon his application to join the Force and I decided that one way would be to actually meet this man. If I turned up at the family hotel in police uniform under some pretext or other he might become suspicious and so it seemed an informal visit was a good idea. At this stage, I kept this information to myself in case I was grossly wrong in considering Groves as a suspect.

On my next weekend off, therefore, I telephoned the Ghylldale Hall Hotel and booked Mary and myself into the restaurant for dinner on the Saturday night, my excuse to Mary being that it was the anniversary of my own appointment to the Force. I didn't even tell her the real reason for my visit even though I was off duty and carrying out this little piece of preliminary detective work on my rest day. When we arrived by taxi, in good time to have an aperitif before eating, I was greeted by a smart young man with just a hint of a misshapen shoulder, and he guided me to the bar, then went behind the counter to dispense the drinks. Dark-haired with a smartly cut style and with grey eyes but no other outstanding facial features, he was dressed in smart dark trousers, polished black shoes, a white shirt with a black bow tie and a neat black velvet jacket. I ordered a sweet sherry for Mary and a malt whisky for myself and we adjourned to a table to enjoy them as we studied the menu. As we did so, other people arrived and suddenly the place became very busy.

One of the nicer features of the hotel was that Mr and Mrs Groves, the owners, were always present as their guests assembled for dinner and they made sure they spoke to each person to wish them an enjoyable meal and pleasant evening. They came to speak to us; I did not tell them I was a police officer but told them we had come from Aidensfield to celebrate an anniversary and the hotel had been recommended by friends. I then asked if the barman was their son. Mr Groves smiled and said, 'You're very observant, Mr Rhea. I'd expect that of a policeman! You are the Aidensfield constable, I believe? I have seen you around the district on occasions. I hope you enjoy your time with us. But yes, he is our son, you can see the likeness, eh? Michael's our only son. He's learning the business but his heart is elsewhere. He's always wanted to be a policeman but he's not tall enough, poor lad. You should see his room, it's full of police things.'

'A collector is he?' I asked, with as much innocent interest as I could muster.

'Badges, buttons, items of uniform, truncheons, photographs of police cars, books about police history, it's all stuff he buys from second-hand shops and some of our customers have given him stuff too, ex-bobbies mainly . . . he even bought one of those high stools that used to be in Eltering Police Station charge office before they modernized it. He found that in a sale-room and got it for a couple of pounds.'

I began to feel something of a heel because Mr Groves had been so kind and forthcoming with his information and clearly, he was very proud of his son, albeit with no idea of his extra-mural policing activities. But he had done enough in my opinion. For another few minutes, he told me about Michael's passion for all things to do with the police, and then went off to chat to another couple.

Mary smiled when he'd gone. 'Why were you encouraging him to chat about his son's collection of police memorabilia? I thought you didn't like police talk when you were off duty?'

'There was a reason,' I tried to sound mysterious. 'I'll tell you when we get home.'

'You're up to something, Nick!' she accused me, but the waiter arrived at just the right time to take our order and permit me to change the subject. But Mary did not forget and once we had left the taxi and gone indoors, the taxi taking our baby-sitter home too, she quizzed me about my reticence in discussing things. I told her the full story with due emphasis on the activities of the bogus constable and I could see she was growing increasingly embarrassed.

'Mary!' I cried, as the full realization struck me. 'You don't mean you got stopped and fined as well?'

'Well, yes, but there's no way I was going to tell you about it!'

'So what happened?' I pressed her.

She said she had been taking a book back to the library in Ashfordly and had rushed to get there just before their doors closed at 5 p.m. one afternoon several weeks earlier, parking her car right outside in the 'No Parking' zone. She'd emerged to find a young constable standing beside her car who had ticked her off and fined her £2, saying it would obviate the need to attend court.

'But there's no such thing as on-the-spot fines!' I reminded her.

'Well, I thought there was, I'd seen something in the paper about them . . .'

'That was about fixed penalty tickets, not on-the-spot fines.' I tried to explain the difference. 'It's all to do with the new traffic warden system . . .'

'I thought he was a traffic warden, he didn't look like a real policeman to me,' she said.

'And yet you parted with a couple of pounds!'

'Well, how was I to know?' she retorted. 'It was an official-looking man in uniform and he gave me a receipt—'

'Did you see him tonight?' I interrupted that spirited defence of her actions.

'Tonight? No, why? Was he hanging around the car park or something?'

'No,' and I paused. 'What about the barman? Could it have been him?'

'The barman?' and she frowned in concentration as she tried to visualize the young barman dressed in police uniform. 'That man behind the bar of the Ghylldale tonight, you mean?'

'Try to imagine him in police uniform,' I suggested. 'Complete with peaked cap and a book of receipts, and looking very official.'

She concentrated on that effort for a few minutes, then said, 'Well, yes, I suppose it could have been him, he did walk rather oddly and the face was similar, but I couldn't swear it was him, Nick. I hope you're not wanting me to go to court over this, are you?'

'I suspect he's our man, Mary, and I need someone to identify him as the uniformed fake constable.'

'Well I couldn't be as sure as that, it was a few weeks ago and it was just a figure in dark-blue uniform; he wasn't nasty or officious, and I was happy to pay up . . . after all, I had parked in the 'No Parking' zone.'

And so our evening concluded. Next morning, I went to see Sergeant Craddock and told him of my experiences. He said he would speak to Inspector Ashton about it before proceeding any further, and consideration would be given to interviewing Michael Groves, along with a search of his room. Later that morning, two detectives paid a visit to Ghylldale Hall Hotel and interviewed Michael, following which they searched his room. They found all manner of police memorabilia including a peaked cap, a tunic without numerals, some highly polished black boots and, more significantly, a few pads of official-looking receipts. They matched the one handed to Clare Milburn.

Faced with that evidence, Michael admitted fining lots of motorists over a period of several weeks, travelling to his scenes in the hotel's van which he used to collect provisions, his only defence being that he thought his victims had been driving badly. He wanted to make them better drivers to stop them knocking down defenceless children—in the manner he had suffered years ago. He did say he was utterly dejected at being refused an appointment with the police and his confession, freely given, was presented to Eltering Magistrates' Court in mitigation when he appeared.

On his own admission, he was found guilty of twenty-two charges of wearing an article of police uniform with intent to deceive, but was fined a total of £100, the maximum for only one offence. He was not charged with any offence of obtaining money by deception—those allegations would 'lie on the table' but he was bound over to be of good behaviour for three years. It was thought these penalties, and the resultant publicity, would prevent him from doing the same thing again.

It appeared to be successful because in spite of the publicity which resulted from Michael's court appearance, we experienced no further cases of false police officers levying fines on unsuspecting motorists. Somewhat surprisingly, I heard a few months later from a colleague in Luton who said that a fake policeman had been fining motorists in his part of the world. It coincided with Michael's departure from the family hotel to pastures unknown and although we passed our information to Luton, I never heard of Michael again. I wonder where he is now? Retired, probably, to enjoy his collection of police memorabilia.

CHAPTER 6

The Teasle twins were young criminals in the making. That was the gospel according to Sergeant Blaketon before he retired. During his service as the sergeant in charge at Ashfordly, he had issued regular warnings to the twins' parents about the lads' propensity for causing upheaval, distress and anger among the local people and at school. In spite of our efforts and those of Mr and Mrs Teasle, Tom and Tim, known widely as the terrible twins, had a long history of trouble-making and mischief in Ashfordly. In spite of that, they had never appeared before the magistrates to answer any charges arising from their unwelcome and anti-social activities.

There were two reasons for this—first, many of their junior exploits occurred away from school and were little more than nuisances committed while the lads were below the age of criminal responsibility. They were regarded as little more than pesky horrors of primary-school age. For such japes, they'd been subjected to warnings from police, parents and neighbours, usually with little impact because each new telling-off seemed to spur them to greater and more imaginative efforts. They thought this ongoing battle was some kind of game. It is not possible to list all their misdemeanours because most never came to the notice of the constabulary, but they included letting down car tyres, unscrewing and hiding the seats of rows of parked pedal cycles, knocking on doors and running away, setting fire prematurely to garden bonfires, cutting the tops off would-be prize vegetables on allotments and opening gates to let hens escape.

One of their highlights was putting buckets of water on the tops of partially opened doors at school to catch unwary teachers who might pass beneath; then they turned to releasing someone's racing pigeons before a big race; hiding neighbours' gardening tools, locking people in outdoor toilets; putting fireworks through letter-boxes and much, much more. On one famous occasion, they removed the ladder of a man who was mending a roof to leave him marooned aloft for several hours and then they used the same ladder to climb on to the roof of a nearby bungalow and place a dustbin lid over the top of a smoking chimney. The sight of the elderly householders rushing out while enveloped in a cloud of choking black smoke was one which had entertained the neighbours for years afterwards.

Even until the time they were around nine or ten years old, such activities were regarded as little worse than humorous pranks. The twins could not understand the anger which sometimes resulted from their actions—for them, of course, it continued to be little more than innocent fun—but they were aware that their age guaranteed them freedom from prosecution. It meant the police held no terrors for the twins, and if any of their victims threatened to call the police, it produced only scorn and laughter. The age of criminal responsibility had been increased to ten in 1963; hitherto, it had been eight. Even with the increase to ten years of age, few children under fourteen were prosecuted unless it could be shown to the court's satisfaction that they knew the consequences of their actions and also knew the difference between right and wrong.

As the twins grew older, their pranks became more daring, more serious and much more troublesome. Indeed, many were criminal offences, such as stealing trinkets from market stalls and running off; taking hens' eggs from the nests and throwing them around; stealing sweets from shops; painting rude words on peoples' garage doors; daubing obscene white-wash slogans on shop windows, smashing the radio aerials of parked motor cars, or stealing their windscreen wipers; making threatening telephone calls to teachers and other people who annoyed them; removing washing from clothes lines; drinking milk waiting on doorsteps, and a host of similarly unwelcome and pointless activities,

As they matured into their early teens, the question of presenting them before a court of law, with sufficient evidence to secure a conviction and so teach them a salutary lesson, became a matter of some importance to Ashfordly Police. Despite the constabulary's best efforts, however, the twins always managed to avoid prosecution and they began to taunt the police about their failures. That brings me to the second reason for their non-appearance in court.

It was simply that they were identical twins. As they had grown older, they had learned to operate separately instead of doing everything together and that meant no one could be sure which twin, if either, had committed the act or crime in question. No longer were the Teasle *twins* the culprit: crimes were committed by just one of them, either Tom or Tim, but no one knew which. In some cases, of course, the witnesses could not be positive as to whether one or other of the twins was truly responsible.

Sometimes, we had nothing more than a vague description of a young man but even if we could not be positive, there were indications that the culprit was one or other of the Teasle twins.

If a police officer went to their home to interview either or both, they would invariably produce an alibi which could be verified. They never admitted anything and on occasions the suspect twin would claim the culprit was his brother, knowing it could never be proved. The brother, of course, always had an alibi. Although it was suspected their alibis were false, we could never prove them to be so; witnesses could never pick out the real suspect when confronted by both lads.

In cases of disputed identification, the twins invariably supported one another with an almost uncanny knack of knowing what the other was thinking or about to say, and not even the most reliable of witnesses, such as police officers, were able to distinguish one from the other. It must be said none of us could be sure to which twin we were speaking. I began to think that each of the twins was known by both names because they always seemed to respond to either and there were even times when I wondered if either of them really knew his *own* correct name.

From a legal point of view, the lack of positive identification of a suspect or offender meant it was unsafe to proceed with a prosecution and certainly no conviction would follow. The maturing twins had come to realize this. It was a logical development of the skills they had developed and nurtured at school—teachers had always mistaken one for the other, with Tim being blamed for acts committed by Tom, and Tom being blamed for acts committed by Tim.

Even when the school had issued them with name badges or coloured armbands in an attempt to distinguish one from the other, they had switched badges or armbands, or else claimed they had done so! No one could ever be quite sure.

So the twins had learned to use their remarkable similarities to great advantage, albeit for very doubtful motives and it was this development which, in the opinion of Sergeant Blaketon, was of increasing concern. He reckoned it was a sure slide towards outright criminality which would continue into their adulthood. He claimed that as the twins had never been halted or punished for committing minor nuisances, they would graduate to more serious matters, inevitably of a criminal nature. He had warned us all about this; he had warned the twins' teachers and their parents; and he'd also warned Tim and Tom themselves.

Blaketon had highlighted the awful penalties that would befall them if they broke the law but the twins continued to think it was all a huge joke. With their animal cunning and skill, they came to believe they could do almost as they liked. Many teenagers boasted that kind of confidence and there were times we knew the lads were deliberately teasing the police, metaphorically raising two fingers at them.

By the time Tom and Tim left school, Sergeant Blaketon had retired from police work and supervision of the Teasle twins had become the responsibility of his successors together with the constables of Ashfordly and a little help from nearby rural bobbies. It is right to say they all tried, with little or no success, to contain the activities of the terrible twins because, as time passed, it was clear that Blaketon's forecast had been right.

Having rampaged unchecked for so long, the twins were turning increasingly to crime with a view of earning easy money—and they were constantly evading arrest because of their remarkable likeness to one another. They took great care never to be actually caught in the act of committing an offence, relying always on escaping from the scene so that any possible witnesses would be confused if the question of identification later arose. In lots of cases, though, the fleeing criminal escaped without witnesses being able to provide a detailed description, certainly not enough to put a name to the suspect, but as the information flowed into our systems, we knew when the culprit was one or other of the Teasle twins—even if we could not prove our theory.

One developing problem was that the maturing twins then made stronger and more determined endeavours to look and behave exactly like one another. As I settled into my brief role as acting sergeant in Ashfordly, they were aged seventeen, five feet ten inches tall with dark hair and brown eyes; they dressed in matching clothes and adopted matching hair styles. When they bought pedal cycles, they were exactly the same style and colour and they even ate the same food in cafés—and even tried to buy the same drinks in pubs even though they were under age. Whatever one of them did to his appearance was emulated quite deliberately and very skilfully by the other. When people said they were like two peas in a pod, it summed up things admirably. They were even more alike than any mirror image.

In maturing adolescence, the twins' similarity continued to be astonishing and it was said that even their parents on occasions, and certainly aunts, uncles, cousins and neighbours found themselves unable to tell one from the other. As acting sergeant, therefore, this was one of the ongoing problems I inherited, if only for a temporary period, and I wondered if there was anything I could do officially to blunt their activities. As I pondered their behaviour, I decided I must try and do something about it so I set aside a period one quiet Wednesday morning in the peace of the sergeant's office at Ashfordly Police Station. I had decided to study the collator's file and anything else we had recorded about the twins over the past years. Because they had never operated on my Aidensfield beat, my personal knowledge of them was fairly slight and based mainly on second-hand information, although I did know them by sight and was aware of their reputation. Rarely had I any occasion to deal with either of them during any of my spells of duty in Ashfordly and so I decided that now, with my new responsibilities, I should learn more about this twin problem.

I was helped by the fact that one of the recent developments within the police service was the role of collator; the system was a good one and right for its time. It worked like this: when officers were patrolling their beats, they would note the date, time and place of all events, however minor, which involved known or suspected criminals; they would record sightings of villains and suspects, the names of those with whom they were seen to be associating, and any other suspicious actions or events likely to be of future interest to the police. At the end of each shift, the officers would present this accumulated intelligence to the collator who would enter it in his card-index system, with rigorous cross-referencing. With a collator at each police station, this proved to be a very important crime-detection and information-gathering system. If a suspected villain's movements had to be traced or checked, it was often possible to track them, their movements and personal contacts through these collators' files. With such a file at every police station, it provided a huge network of useful facts and this kind of positive crime-busting information, recorded in writing, could, among other things, either make or break a suspect's alibi. Long-serving officers like Alf Ventress had a wealth of crime-beating information tucked away in their brains; this new system placed that kind of valuable information on paper for the benefit of all. Every scrap of crime-beating intelligence within that system was made readily available to every police officer, both in local police and further afield.

From those files, therefore, I learned that the twins had left school about a year previously and were now seventeen, with both in work. Here there was an important difference. Tom was employed by a builder where he was learning brick-laying skills at sites within the region, and Tim worked for a soft-drinks manufacturer, working in the warehouse despatch department, arranging deliveries of crates of lemonade and fruit juice and dealing with orders from pubs, clubs, restaurants and shops. I believe he was very efficient at this. Both lads continued to live at home. Their respective jobs meant they worked regular hours with evenings and weekends free. This provided ample time for mischief but it was usually something of a local nature because, at that stage, their only mode of personal transport, when not at work, was the pedal cycle. Neither had a motor bike or car, and they seemed to avoid, where possible, the use of public transport. And, of course, one twin on a pedal cycle looked exactly like the other twin on an identical pedal cycle. The files did not reveal any wrongdoing by either twin at their places of work, although we knew that most commercial organizations dealt internally with dishonest staff. The fact that neither twin was sacked suggested they were behaving honestly at work, or possibly that they'd never been caught fiddling.

Away from work, however, it was a different story. Listed in our files were several instances where one or other of the twins had been suspected or known to have been engaged in criminal activities in Ashfordly or nearby towns. From this information, we began to gather proof that they were changing their tactics. Instead of committing childish crimes such as shoplifting from chain stores, vandalism and ransacking allotments, they were developing into much more sophisticated operators. It did not take long to establish their *modus operandi* even if we lacked the necessary evidence to secure a conviction or even bring them before a court. One of their tactics was this—one of the twins would rush into a shop which dealt mainly in cash sales and grab a fistful of notes before galloping to freedom to get lost among the crowds of shoppers. While this was happening, the other innocent twin would endeavour to be some distance from the scene of the crime always making sure he had an alibi which coincided with the time of the crime.

When an officer went to interview Tim, he would say 'Oh, it wasn't me, officer, I have an alibi, just you go and have a word with—' and he would name the witness. If he interviewed Tom, he could say the same thing; he would also produce a firm alibi with the same witness. If both were seen some distance from the scene of the crime at the time it occurred, how could either be guilty? Thus both twins were seen to have alibis. No court would deliver a guilty verdict in such a case.

Most of the police officers at Ashfordly suspected that one of these alibis was false, but the snag was that the witnesses had no idea to whom they had really been speaking except that it was either Tim or Tom—or both. Poring over the files, with special attention to the timing of the crimes and the supposed alibis, I began to see a glimmer of light in the way the twins operated.

In my opinion, it was clear that one twin would commit a crime at a pre-arranged time while the other created an alibi for both. He did this by speaking to two alibi witnesses some distance from the scene of the crime and with a few minutes between each chat. He would use one name, say Tim, when speaking to the first witness, and Tom's name when speaking to the second witness. Then I realized the twin even had the nerve to speak to the same alibi witness on two occasions while using both names. If this was true, it was pushing their luck rather too far but it revealed the confidence they possessed. Thus the witness or witnesses thought they had seen both twins at the alibi time, whereas they had really just seen one of them on two separate but very close occasions, say fifteen minutes apart. And while those alibis were being established, a crime was being committed some distance away.

As I pored over the files, this technique became increasingly evident. In two of the cases, I noted, the twins had been logged chatting to a policeman in Ashfordly at the very time a cash snatch had been effected at a newsagent's shop in Brantsford, some eight miles away. Happily, PC Alwyn Foxton, the constable in question, had recorded in some detail those visits by the twins. Tom had been the first and fifteen minutes later, he had recorded a chat to the second twin, Tim. On the face of things, this sounded very much like an unshakeable alibi, but as I thought more about it, I remembered this pair loved to taunt the police in a variety of ways. Had Alwyn seen the same man twice, once as himself and once pretending to be his brother? I would have to speak to him about it. I began to wonder whether this brief and deliberate taunting of a policeman might indeed be the undoing of the Teasle twins.

I continued this modest research wondering if there was any other pattern or routine to their criminal activities. Were the crimes committed at a certain time of day perhaps? Could I adopt the Target Criminal technique of having them observed over a long period with a view to logging their every movement and contact? The problem was I did not have sufficient officers at my disposal to justify full-time observations of that kind and as police officers worked shifts, it also meant I could not guarantee that a particular policeman would be in the same place at the same time each day or even each week to monitor the twins' movements.

I guessed they travelled to their crime scenes by cycle too; it was the only transport they used for we knew they did not use public transport, so although their mode of transport was slow, it provided considerable freedom of movement. It offered much more scope for evading the police than the local bus service. For a fit young man, a cycle ride from Ashfordly to Brantsford would take about half an hour at the most, I thought, while the Ashfordly to Eltering run would be around an hour—that's if they used the main road. I began to think we could monitor those routes to see whether either of the twins cycled that way, or indeed to any other destination, at any particular time, To reach Eltering by the main road, they would have to pass through Brantsford, although the minor lanes, maze-like in their complexity, offered a bewildering selection of alternative routes.

The information in the files produced several other factors. One was that the unsolved crimes for which the twins were currently suspected were all committed on a Saturday afternoon, usually within an hour of the targeted premises closing—a time when the tills would be full. In all cases, only cash in notes was stolen—pound notes and ten-shilling notes were far lighter to carry than coins, and very easy to dispose of. On a few occasions, they even managed to steal a five-pound note or two.

No violence was ever used against the shopkeepers or their assistants—it was literally a swift seizure of a single fistful of notes from an all-too-conveniently placed till, often while the assistant's attention was momentarily distracted by another customer. As many tills were placed near the doors to cope with customers as they left the premises, they presented easy pickings for fast-moving, daring criminals of this kind. The thieves could snatch the money and be away from the premises in seconds, leaving the assistant wondering whether to risk giving chase and thus leave the shop vulnerable to further attack, or ring in the police in the hope an officer might be somewhere in the vicinity. Invariably, the assistants stayed with the shop and rang the police by which time the villain had made good his escape with the flustered assistant gaining only a glimpse of the fleeing raider.

I noticed there were no references to the suspects using pedal cycles for their escapes either, but on most occasions, the witness's descriptions failed to provide sufficient detail for a positive identification. That was very understandable because these incidents happened so quickly while generating a great deal of shock and anxiety. In some cases, it was surprising we got any kind of description of the suspect. Another factor in the twins' favour was that even if the raider did get stopped and searched, how could anyone prove the notes in his possession had come from the attacked premises? The only way to prove the notes in his possession had been stolen was for them to be marked in some way, or have their serial numbers recorded. In that way, we might prove their true ownership, but if we were to plant notes in anticipation of a raid, we would have to know their next target premises— which we did not. Our crime prevention teams, however, did visit all the attacked premises and those which had, to date, escaped the attention of the raider, and gave suitable advice, such as not allowing the tills to become full near closing time—the money could always be removed to a safer place—or to relocate their tills deeper inside the premises, or even to lodge a marked note or two permanently in the till.

In the latter case, a marked note could remain in the till just in case it was ever raided and the culprit caught in possession of the suspect cash. To catch a thief with an identifiable note in his possession was extremely valuable evidence, ideal for presenting to the court. We hoped the owners of all vulnerable premises would co-operate with us in that way.

I checked some twenty unsolved cases which had been recorded over a period of a year; in all cases, the twins had been suspected and interviewed, and in all cases both had an alibi. One odd factor which emerged was that several of the more recent alibi witnesses had been policemen—that was a very cheeky ploy and seemed to be one of their favourites because it placed the law on their side! It was a daring means of teasing the police too, but if a police officer could provide an alibi for a suspect, who would argue against that? Other alibis they'd used were visiting pubs, snooker halls, football matches, doing cash-in-hand work for someone—anything which could be checked and verified, but always with people who were unable to positively identify one twin from another. They thought they'd seen both twins whereas I believed they'd seen only one. Clever stuff, I thought. But not clever enough.

Before taking further action, though, I felt I must speak to PC Alwyn Foxton to see if he could recall precisely what had transpired during his chat with the 'twins'. He was on duty in the town as I was poring over those files and so, to benefit from a break in my studies with a walk in the fresh air, I put on my cap and went to meet him.

After explaining my theories, I asked, 'Can you remember exactly what was said that day, Alwyn?'

'Yes, I took great care with this because I knew the twins' reputation. One of them approached me as I was in the market square, in Ashfordly. It was half past four on a Saturday afternoon as near as dammit and he asked if I'd seen his brother. I knew the twins well enough by sight, we all did. I asked him "So which one are you?" He told me he was Tom Teasle, and that his brother was somewhere in town, and he wondered if I'd seen him. I hadn't seen either twin prior to that encounter and I said so. "If you see Tim," said Tom. "Tell him I'm looking for him. I'll be in the snooker hall till five, and then I'll go straight home." I assured him I would pass on the message if I saw his brother and off he went, smiling. He didn't have his bike with him, by the way, or if he did, he'd parked it somewhere out of sight.'

'Right. So he said he was Tom, but was he really Tom?' I asked.

'I've no idea, I just knew he was one of the twins, but I knew about them being suspected of crimes so I made a note in my pocket-book. My idea was to enter it into the collator's files when I got back to the office, just in case he was up to some trickery. Which I'm sure he was!'

'And then?'

'Well, Nick, ten minutes or a quarter of an hour later, something like that, I thought he was heading for me again, but this one said, "Excuse me, Constable, I'm looking for my brother, you might know him, Tom Teasle. I wondered if you had seen him in town?" I thought I'd play him along so I said, "You must be Tim, then?" and he smiled and said yes. I then told him Tom was in the snooker hall and he said he'd go and find him. I made a note of that visit in my pocket-book. Later, of course, I heard about the raid at Brantsford and although the description of the raider was rather vague, it could have fitted either of the twins and so I told CID. They interviewed both of them at home and both said they had spoken to me around half past four that day, and although I told CID I thought they were having me on, with one man doing the alibi for both, they said they couldn't break it and so we had no evidence against them. But I think they'd been doing that sort of thing for some time, Nick, one man creating alibis for both while the other was carrying out the raid some distance away. There's no wonder we could never pin anything on them.'

'Thanks, Alwyn, I agree with you, but how can we nail them? That's the problem; we can't let it go without trying to do something. Leave it with me, I've got to give this a lot of thought; the laws of evidence don't seem to have catered for this kind of thing!'

Alwyn Foxton, a policeman of many years' service, was pleased someone was listening to his suspicions; he had the impression the CID weren't all that interested in his theory, thinking perhaps that Alwyn was making up a most unlikely scenario out of a perfectly innocent event, but I supported him.

If one twin was producing alibis for both, either by talking to one witness or two, then there must be some means of breaking their cover story. In the days that followed, I went to Brantsford Police Station and Eltering Sub-Divisional Headquarters and examined the crime reports in their systems in addition to all those in Ashfordly's records, trying to identify every crime within the past year which had probably been committed by one of the Teasle twins.

What emerged was that most of the shop assistants working in the attacked premises, or witnesses who chanced to be in the nearby streets at the time, were unable to provide positive identifications of the suspects. For every snatch crime, the descriptions loosely fitted one of the Teasle twins even if no positive identification could be made, and I had to be honest with myself and say such descriptions could fit hundreds of local men. When I checked the collators' files in each of those police stations, several policemen had logged chats with one or both of the twins at the time of the snatches—and noted the clothing they had been wearing. In all cases, they had been some distance from the scene of the crime, too far for the guilty party to have covered in the available time. Even so, a strong pattern was definitely emerging.

When I interviewed the constables concerned, they all said the same thing—they had been warned to look out for the twins and to log all their movements, but some had not thought to log the second chat, believing the story about one twin looking for the other to be honest. When I explained what had happened to Alwyn Foxton, the penny dropped. We were being cleverly used to provide alibis for a long-running series of crimes and most of the officers to whom I spoke could recall a second unsuspicious visit by the 'brother'. Our task, now we had uncovered their ploy, was to catch them with enough evidence to prove our theory. It seemed the only way was to set a trap. For that, we would have to determine the venue of a forthcoming raid—and we would also have to break their alibi with sufficient authority and enough evidence to be acceptable in a court of law.

And, I knew, if the twins were taken to court, they'd play their 'likeness' card to good effect—all they had to do was to cast doubt on the police evidence of identification. The tiniest doubt would result in an acquittal.

By chance, I spotted a fortuitous opportunity. It was the appointment of two constables whose names appeared in General Orders as they were being posted to their stations after their three months of initial training. One was PC 362 Daniel Whitworth and the other was PC 263 David Whitworth. Having once worked closely with members of the recruiting department, I knew how their minds worked—two constables with similar names and almost identical numbers on their shoulders? Could they possibly be twins? I felt I had to ring to find out. When I spoke to Sergeant Collins, the recruiting sergeant, he confirmed my belief.

'The Whitworth twins, Nick, yes. Identical they are. They gave their training-school instructors a right old runaround, I can tell you. They never knew which was which . . . imagine staging a traffic accident with one of the twins being the driver and the other the constable who has to interview him . . . and then they had to switch roles for training purposes. They never knew who really had done both tasks. I'm glad we've got them through that stage! We had to separate them, though, we couldn't do with the public being as confused as our training-school sergeants were!'

'So where are they now?' I asked.

'One's been posted to Scarborough and the other's gone to Whitby. We couldn't let them loose in the same town.'

'And are they identical?' I asked.

'Like peas in a pod!' laughed Sergeant Collins. 'And ginger haired with it! Freckles and ginger hair, and a ginger moustache, both of them, brown eyes . . . you'd think you were looking at a mirror image. Why are you asking all this, Nick?'

I explained about the troublesome Teasle twins and said I was wondering if there was any possible way in which I could make use of these twin policemen to set a trap for the Teasles.

'That's not for me, Nick!' chuckled Collins. 'You'll have to speak to their respective divisional commanders about it, but I can't see how you can use these ginger twins, they cause nothing but confusion when they're together.'

'Thanks, Sarge,' I said. 'At least I know they're identical, and if they cause trouble because of that, they'll know how the Teasles think and behave. I could use a bit of that kind of guile! I'll consider it further before I do anything, but thanks for your help.'

'Good luck,' he laughed, and rang off.

I had no power to draft these ginger-moustached twin constables to Ashfordly on a mere whim of mine, so I knew I must establish a sound case for requesting their presence. My arguments had to be strong enough to convince two divisional commanders and probably a few cynical detectives into the bargain. I set about studying the facts all over again, trying to determine how the Teasle twins determined their targets, when they were likely to strike again and any other salient feature of their operations. I decided to concentrate upon their raids in Brantsford, this market town being regularly targeted by them.

At least six attacks had been recorded there, all snatches from cash tills shortly before closing time, and all suspects' descriptions being very similar to one or other of the twins. And then I spotted something else of significance. Those six snatches had all occurred during the past year, and each one had been on the last Saturday of the month, around 4.30 p.m. But the raids had not been carried out throughout the year, they had happened only in May, June, July, August, September and October. There had been no raid in November, December, January, February or March. And we were now in April . . . suppose they resumed this coming May? That gave me a few weeks to work out some kind of strategy, but how could I be sure the raids would resume in May? And why select those summer months? The other crimes had been committed in Eltering and even Ashfordly during the winter, but why pick those summer months for crimes in Brantsford?

Wednesday was the normal market-day in Brantsford, but a minor secondary market had developed on Saturdays which meant the small town grew busy with locals, tourists and visitors alike, some coming for the shopping, some coming to see the touristy sights and others arriving especially for the Saturday market which specialized in vegetables and fruit. That was an all-the-year-round event, however, and not restricted to the summertime. But it gave me the necessary clue. During the summer, other events generated larger crowds, so what sort of thing happened on the last Saturday of those months? The events diary, kept in the sergeant's office and used by him when compiling the duty sheets, might provide the answer. And so it did.

Tucked away along a lane near the top of Brantsford marketplace was Brantsford Hall, the stately home of Lord and Lady Brantsford. The house and grounds were open to the public from Easter until the end of September but the grounds only were open during October too. The Hall staged various open-air events throughout the summer, always on the last Saturday of the month and our diary showed there had been a traction engine rally, an antiques fair, a vintage motor cycle rally, a vintage car rally, an art and crafts fair and a country fair with clay-pigeon shooting, angling contests, sheep dog trials and so forth. In all cases, the police were told of the events, even though they were on private premises, but our interest was the traffic they generated in town, and any crimes which might be committed during the event. We did not patrol the grounds or involve ourselves with car-parking on the premises; for that kind of thing, stewards were employed. Our main area of responsibility lay on the public roads unless, of course, a crime was committed. So why did these snatch raids occur during those particular weekends? Was it because the little town became extra busy as the Hall was discharging its visitors around 4.30 p.m.? Certainly, a large crowd would swamp the town with people, cars and coaches as the Hall's visitors departed, or was it just a coincidence that the raids occurred around that time? Or was it because one of the Teasle twins attended these events—or was a steward there? Was that the reason for his presence in Brantsford at that time? I began to see a glimmer of light in this case and bent to my task.

Never during any of our interviews with the Teasle twins had they mentioned Brantsford Hall: I would have thought that if they'd been employed there as, say, part-time car-parking attendants or stewards, they'd have referred to that in one or more of their alibis. As they had never done this, I wondered if it was the presence of large numbers of people in town on such occasions which attracted them to Brantsford's tiny marketplace? After all, even three or four busloads of pensioners would create a crowd in tiny Brantsford—and it only needed a modest crowd near a targeted shop if a villain was to escape. Nonetheless, I checked with the Hall's secretary to see whether they had the name of Teasle in the records they used to recruit part-time staff for their open days, but was assured no such name was on their lists. I began to feel that one of them might visit such an event as an additional cover story if the alibi pretext ever failed. Then there was the question of his cycle. Where did he leave it? None of the witnesses had mentioned a cycle being used.

But whatever I discovered, there was no guarantee it would lead to the apprehension of a guilty Teasle twin, consequently there was an element of risk to whatever scheme I devised. Hundreds of police exercises were staged every year without results but sometimes one did work very well. For all the risks involved, I felt I should start the procedures which would lead to an exercise in Ashfordly and Brantsford on the last Saturday in May, an exercise designed to arrest one or other of the Teasle twins if a crime was committed within, or in striking distance of, the two towns.

I went for a long walk on the moors where I was out of contact for a couple of hours for I wanted to think through the whole idea without interruption before making my approach to the inspector, and when I was ready, I drove through to Eltering for a meeting, having telephoned in advance to make an appointment. When I arrived for the 11 a.m. meeting in mid-April, I was shown to Inspector Breckon's office and, when I entered, Detective Sergeant Howard Bedford was also there. Breckon was a pleasant man who had arranged coffee for us and he then asked me to outline my proposal. I provided a detailed account of the twins' activities and added details of my own research; Bedford added his own comments which supported my account for his men had been trying to pin down the twins with some positive identification.

'So Nick,' smiled Inspector Breckon. 'What are you proposing?'

I knew I had to present my suggestions in a positive way, to make them believe me and to persuade them to back my judgement.

'We need to stage an operation, sir, at two locations, Brantsford and Ashfordly and we need to do so on the last Saturday of May, the twenty-seventh,' and I explained the reason for selecting that date. 'We need to cover the period around 4.30 p.m. Brantsford will be busy, there's the annual traction engine rally at Brantsford Hall, and it always brings lots of extra people into town. There are bus trips and enthusiasts as well the normal weekend activity, shoppers and so on; it's market-day too. I expect one of the twins to stage a robbery, sir, a snatch of cash from one of the town-centre shops. He'll do so around 4.30 p.m. when the till is full, grab a fistful of cash and run for it. I have no idea which shop it will be, that's the unfortunate thing, except I anticipate a small shop dealing only in cash, one with a till near the exit door. There are plenty of those in town, sir, newsagents, sweet shops, small cafés, greengrocers, butcher, bread shop and so on. We need a police presence in Brantsford, sir, in plain clothes, and quite separate from duties at the traction engine rally. We need someone who knows the twins by sight, who can spot one of them among the crowds, note what he is wearing and shadow him without being spotted.'

'To make an arrest?' smiled Bedford, 'Or are you suggesting we let him go and follow him?'

'Ideally to make an arrest, Sergeant, we need to catch him in possession of the money, and positive evidence to link him to the crime. Police observations and continuity of evidence should do that, if we can achieve it without losing him. If he gets away—which has happened every time so far—we need someone to get ahead of him and await his return home.

By then, of course, the second twin should also be home and so the whole question of identification of the real villain will arise once more, with the second twin producing the joint alibi he's concocted that same afternoon—and we won't be able to prove that any money in the possession of one twin was in fact the stolen cash.'

'That's been our problem all along, Nick, without proof that he's in possession of the proceeds of the crime we can't go to court, so how do you propose to deal with that?' asked Breckon.

'We run a second operation in tandem at Ashfordly, sir, during the time of the anticipated raid. One of the twins will, I believe, approach someone in Ashfordly at the time of the planned raid; he'll make sure that person knows who he is and will give his name. He'll say he's expecting to meet his brother, and he'll specify a place such as the snooker hall, cricket field or bookies' shop. When that happens, we'll know the raid is on—it might even have been committed at that stage, or very near to it. Because he's been in the habit of using policemen as his alibi witnesses, I suggest we ensure there's an officer in uniform in the marketplace at the material time. It's almost a hundred per cent certain that a Teasle will approach him.'

'Fair enough, that seems sensible; it's a pity we don't have personal radio sets, I've heard they're being developed but not in operational use just yet, if we had such a thing, we could liaise, but go on, Nick. Tell us more of this grand plan.'

'A few minutes later after the first twin has established his presence, the "second" one will approach the same constable, he'll give the other name and say he's looking for his brother, and will expect the constable to direct him to the aforementioned place to find his "brother". As we know, it will be the same twin adopting both roles, Tim and Tom, but it establishes an alibi for both.'

'Right, fair enough. I've got that. So what are you proposing? How can we break that alibi? We've tried in the past.'

'By using PCs David and Daniel Whitworth, sir; they're identical twin constables with ginger hair and ginger moustaches, one's at Whitby and the other's at Scarborough. Their likeness caused mayhem at training school, sir, so we borrow them for this operation. We position one of them in Ashfordly marketplace before half past four that Saturday; one of the twins will approach him to say he's looking for his brother and he'll then provide Whitworth with his own destination. When he does that, sir, we'll know the raid is on, but the constable must then return to the police station as fast as he can, without Teasle realizing, to let us know the raid is being staged—and that Whitworth constable will be immediately replaced by his twin lookalike brother. When the Teasle twin returns ten or fifteen minutes later in the guise of his own brother, he'll not notice the difference in the constables but will give a different name while believing he's speaking to the same policeman. But in this case, our second constable doesn't let him get away—he arrests him and brings him to the police station before he can alert his real brother, the one who has been executing the raid in Brantsford. In the police station, the arrested twin will be questioned about his alibi. He's bound to say he spoke to a constable and we will then ask him to identify the constable to whom he spoke. When his brother returns home, he will also claim he had an alibi in Ashfordly—he knows his brother will have fixed it—but at that stage he cannot know about the ginger-moustached constable. He'll just be able to say he spoke to a policeman, a lie of course. We can put both twins on the spot by asking them to identify the constable in question.'

'You've lost me now, Nick,' sighed Bedford. 'I can't see why we need to go through all this palaver, all we need to do is arrest the Ashfordly twin before he has a chance to alert his brother.'

'It's a question of undermining their confidence, sir,' I said. 'And by proving both are using false alibis, we can prosecute them for conspiracy; the ingredients are all there. The Ashfordly twin won't be able to alert his brother to the identity of the constable to whom "both" spoke—all the raider-twin has to say is that he spoke to a constable and can't remember what he looked like. The one who *did* speak to the constable will remember him and we can ask him to make an identification.'

'By producing a ginger-moustached policeman?'

'By producing two ginger-moustached policemen, sir, who look just like two peas in a pod. That way, we can confuse him. If he loses his cool, he won't remember which name he gave to which constable, he won't be able to make his alibi stand and that means we've got him. And with the constable in question being new to the town, Teasle will make sure he remembers Teasle . . .'

'It seems a bit over the top for me, sir,' admitted Bedford.

'I can see what Nick's getting at,' smiled Breckon. 'It might just work . . . I vote we give it a try, Howard. Let's face it, we've nothing to lose and a lot to gain. And I bet our constable twins' minds operate just like the Teasle twins—I've heard they had their training sergeants running around like headless chickens; they know all the tricks of being identical.'

'The Teasles have given us a right run-around over the last year or more . . . so if we can get those ginger lookalikes, yes, I'll go along with it, it'll be a laugh if nothing else! At least it means we're doing something positive about those raids—and we might even get a conviction out of all this!'

'Right,' said Inspector Breckon. 'I'll see about arranging for those two constables to attend one of our preliminary meetings. There should be no problems securing them for an operational exercise of this kind.'

And so we began our work on Operation Double Deal.

The snag with planning operations of this kind is that no matter how hard and carefully one prepares, something can always go wrong, some unforeseen problem, but having considered all the likely areas of difficulty, the scheme was set up. The respective divisional commanders allowed the twin Whitworth constables to be attached temporarily to Ashfordly for the operation and indeed, they were sent a couple of days early to familiarize themselves with the locality.

In arranging their duties for those preliminary days, I had to make sure both twins were fully briefed about the Teasle twins' life and work, and that they recognized them. This had to be done without the Teasles being aware of any kind of surveillance and also without the ginger constables appearing together on the streets, even in civilian clothes. All that was achieved successfully and so, with all our preparations in place, Saturday, 25 May dawned.

A detective constable from Eltering, DC Chris Paget, who was a keen cyclist, was given the task of observing the scene in Brantsford around 4.30 p.m.; he'd familiarized himself with the Teasle twins' appearance and had even cycled past their home in Ashfordly. His duty therefore was to maintain a presence in the centre of Brantsford, along with his cycle and dressed in cycling gear. He was to monitor any movements of Tim or Tom Teasle and if possible, try to calculate which of the many little shops would be the Teasle target for today. He had to do his best to maintain contact with Brantsford Police Station without Teasle becoming suspicious of his activities and, if possible, he had to arrest Teasle in the act. We were also interested to learn where Teasle concealed his cycle during the raid. It was a tall order—it meant being on the spot at the very moment the crime was committed; if he failed, then he had to try and find Teasle who would be using his bike at some point, and shadow him to his home at Ashfordly. We needed proof that this Teasle was not at home that day, that he was not in Ashfordly marketplace at the time of the crime and that he did not speak to a constable, or in any other way attempt to establish an alibi. And, of course, we had to try and determine which of the Teasles was the raider.

DC Paget seemed confident enough to cope with this task and with any unexpected developments that would surely arise. He would be supported by DC Sharpe in a plain police vehicle parked close to the Teasle home in Ashfordly. That officer would monitor the comings-and-goings from the Teasle household and of course, he had the benefit of a police radio in the car.

Meanwhile in Ashfordly, PC 362 David Whitworth, in full uniform, would be patrolling the town centre which included the market square. He would be on duty there from 2 p.m. onwards, but had been ordered to ensure he was in the square from 4 p.m. until 5 p.m. He was told to make himself prominent, not to get lost among tourists and shoppers. He had to wait until a Teasle twin approached him and record the exact words used by the twin (but not with the twin being aware of it), and immediately Teasle was out of sight, David must hurry to Ashfordly Police Station, a walk of two or three minutes. As he appeared in sight of the station windows, so his brother Daniel would walk out in full uniform to take his brother's place in the market square. He had also to wait until a Teasle twin approached him, remember his exact words, then arrest him and convey him to the police station. That would be the first shock element of this exercise. In the station, the Teasle twin would be interrogated by Detective Sergeant Bedford—the power of arrest came from the suspicion of conspiracy, and the fact that a Teasle had approached the constable was good evidence that a crime had been perpetrated by the brother in Brantsford. Or so we hoped.

While this double operation was going ahead, the rest of us had to proceed with our duties in as normal a manner as possible, and so it was, that at 4 p.m. that Saturday, I was sitting in the sergeant's office wondering if it had all been a big mistake, whether the Teasles would rise to the occasion and commit a crime, whether they would defeat us yet again, and thus all my efforts might be in vain. Howard Bedford was with me, as was PC Daniel Whitworth. We could do little but wait. Ashfordly police office was staffed by PC Alf Ventress in clouds of cigarette smoke and at Brantsford's enquiry counter there was PC Dick Hebron, both of whom had been well briefed about the day's anticipated events.

And so we waited and waited. Time seemed to move ever so slowly and then things began to happen. The phone rang and Ventress snatched it from the rest.

'Right,' he said after a few moments. 'Thanks,' and replaced it.

'Dick Hebron at Brantsford, Sarge,' he addressed both Bedford and me with Daniel listening in. 'There's been a snatch, a couple of minutes ago. Half past four as near as dammit. At a dry-cleaners. Thirty or forty quid thought to be missing in pound notes and ten bob notes, all used. The suspect matches the general description of a Teasle—slim build, dark hair, about eighteen year old or so, wearing a navy-blue jumper and blue jeans. No mention of a bike, he ran off down an alley next to the cleaners and vanished before anyone could catch him. Paget was nearby at the time but couldn't get to him . . . Brantsford beat bobbies are searching the town and Hebron will inform DC Sharpe who's waiting near the Teasle home.'

'Thanks, Alf,' I said. 'So I wonder if the other Teasle has made contact with PC Whitworth?'

And at this point, the young constable could be seen hurrying to the police station.

'You're on your way,' I said to Daniel. 'Here comes your David.'

David burst in, panting and said, 'He's been, Sarge, like you said. Four twenty-six to be precise. Tom Teasle he called himself. He realized I was new here and introduced himself, shook my hand, then said he was looking for his brother; he said he'd be in the town hall, there's a flea-market going on in there. Would I send his brother in to meet him there if he asked.'

'Well done. Right, Daniel. Off you go. If a Teasle comes to you, he should call himself Tim. So I wonder which one we have in Brantsford?'

And off went Daniel—at least I think it was Daniel—while David joined us. We explained the raid had occurred, the thief had escaped as we had expected and a hunt was now in progress in Brantsford, eight miles away. There was nothing we could do to help our colleagues there but the phone rang again. It was Paget and he asked to speak to DS Bedford.

Bedford listened and then told us, 'Paget was about twenty-five yards away; he'd spotted Teasle in the town centre and was shadowing him but just before half past four Teasle hurried into the gents and, when he didn't emerge, Paget went too, ostensibly to relieve himself but discovered there were two exits, front and back. Teasle had gone out the back way. Paget hurried outside and was in time to see Teasle enter the dry-cleaners and almost immediately run out again, but was too far away to arrest him. Teasle—and he's sure it was one of the Teasles—escaped down an alleyway, one of many in Brantsford, and Paget gave chase along with several other people, but by the time they all got to the end of the alley, Teasle had vanished. Paget thinks he had his bike waiting there. The alley opens on to a lane which runs behind the town-centre shops; its full of sheds, outside toilets, garages, back entrances to shops and warehouses, that sort of thing . . . so Paget will now cycle towards Ashfordly. He hopes he might be lucky enough to see Teasle *en route*! Brantsford's bobbies are making the normal enquiries and are conducting a search of the town centre.'

'Can't we stage a road block between Brantsford and here?' asked Bedford. 'He'll have to pass through at some stage.'

'Not necessarily,' I reminded him. 'There's a whole network of minor roads between here and Brantsford. There are several routes he could take, well away from normal traffic. I would think he'd avoid the main route, even if using the side roads means it takes longer.'

'Fair enough, point taken, Nick. Anyway, we'll catch him when he comes home, even if we can't prove he took the cash. We've enough evidence to link him to the job anyway, thanks to Paget, so we can always use the conspiracy charge.'

Fifteen minutes later, as we hung around to pass the time in the enquiry office, Daniel Whitworth arrived with a protesting Teasle twin in a firm armlock; fortunately, Bedford saw them approaching and snapped to David Whitworth, 'Into the sergeant's office quickly, lad. Keep out of sight; we'll call you soon . . .'

Daniel thrust the protesting youth into the police office as Alf Ventress moved to stand in the doorway, thus preventing any escape. I noticed Teasle was wearing blue jeans and a plain red jumper. 'Tim Teasle, Sarge,' panted Daniel, as he released the struggling Teasle.

'Hello, Tim,' smiled DS Bedford, 'What have you been up to?'

'Up to? Nothing! I just went to this copper and asked if he'd seen my brother and he arrests me . . . what have I done? Tell me that. It's a bad day when innocent people can't go about their business without being arrested. I want a solicitor.'

'So are you Tim or Tom?'

'Tim,' snapped the Teasle.

'And where's Tom?' asked Bedford.

'In town somewhere, he said he'd meet me there.'

'And how did you arrange to find each other?'

'Like we've always done: we tell a constable. We often do it. We saw the constable in the marketplace, this one here, the new chap, and Tom said he would tell the constable where he was going so I could join him later.'

'What time was that?'

'Just after two. We walked into the town centre from home.'

'So you claim you both saw this constable in the town centre at two?'

'We did, I'll swear to it.'

'Did you speak to him then?'

'No, later, just now, when I asked about my brother.'

'PC Whitworth, were you in Ashfordly town centre at two this afternoon?' asked Bedford slyly.

'No, Sergeant, I didn't get there until just after four-thirty.'

'He's lying . . . you're trying to set me up for something . . . he was there, I saw him.'

'*You* saw him? Or was it Tom who saw him?'

'I saw him, we both saw him, we made our arrangements . . . he was there . . . look, I don't know what's going on here but I saw that constable in the town centre at two when me and Tom arrived.'

'And I say you are lying, Tim. This constable was not in the town at that time.'

I could see that Tim was growing uncomfortable by this development and the expression on his face revealed his anxiety, but Bedford did not produce the solution just yet. He went on, 'Tim, suppose I tell you that Tom has never been in Ashfordly this afternoon. He's been to Brantsford. Raiding a dry-cleaner's in fact. And observed by our officers who are, this very minute, tailing him.'

'He can't have, he was here in town with me till we parted and decided to meet up . . . that copper can prove it . . . Look, you can't kid me like this . . . you, that ginger copper, you've got to tell them the truth. Tom said he would speak to the copper about half-four to say where I was . . . so we've both talked to him.'

PC Daniel Whitworth looked into Tim's eyes and said, 'Tim, Mr Teasle, I was not in Ashfordly marketplace at two this afternoon. I was not there before four-thirty either. I am prepared to swear that in a court of law. I arrived just after half past four, a few minutes before Mr Teasle approached me.'

'All right, you're lying, you're setting me up for something. I'll not say another word. I want a solicitor.'

'PC Whitworth?' called Bedford and PC David made his appearance. We all watched as Tim's eyes moved in disbelief from one ginger-moustached constable to the other and then David did a most unexpected thing.

'Hello, Mr Teasle,' he smiled, in a welcoming way. 'Nice to see you again,' and he held out his hand for Teasle to shake. Tim reacted automatically.

He shook hands—and at that instant, he realized his mistake. It had taken the skills of one identical twin to recognize a possible weakness in another.

'I was sure you hadn't met this constable,' smiled Bedford. 'I thought you'd met his brother, this man here.'

'I was talking about two o'clock . . .'

'No,' snapped Bedford. 'We are talking about half past four or thereabouts. You pretended to be Tom at that point, and you met this PC Whitworth; a few minutes later you met his brother, this time calling yourself Tim.'

'Right, Sergeant,' smiled David. 'This man is Tom all right. He was Tom when he shook my hand just before four-thirty and even though he says he's Tim now, I know he's Tom. Tom is a builder, he's got builder's hands, all rough and hard . . .'

'So, Tom, if you have been masquerading as yourself and your brother this afternoon, what's your brother been up to? I think we shall soon know the answer. All right, put him in the cells for now, strip all harmful objects from him and I'll charge him with conspiracy. And I shall have your fingerprints taken, Tom. Even if you are identical twins, your fingerprints will be different. That distinction will be most useful to have in our files.'

Tim, having discarded his blue sweater in favour of a red jumper, was caught later that day as he arrived home. He was in possession of a marked pound note too; happily, the manager of the dry-cleaner's had heeded our earlier crime prevention advice and had planted a marked note in the till, just in case of a robbery. That was a bonus for us, and it meant we could prove the case against Tim.

The twins appeared at Ashfordly Magistrates' Court, each charged with conspiracy to steal, and Tim was also charged with theft.

Both were sent to Quarter Sessions for trial and found guilty; we could not prove their guilt for the previous offences and they never admitted any other crimes. They were each given a sentence of six months suspended for three years, which meant that if they committed a further serious crime within that three years, the six-month sentence would be activated in addition to any other penalty. And of course, we now had their fingerprints on record. I just hoped they were recorded in their correct names.

And the relevance of the events at Brantsford Hall? Although we could never prove it, we knew it was Tim who carried out all the raids in Brantsford, and Tom who used police officers to establish their alibis under the two names. Whenever there was an event in the Hall grounds, Tim would cycle there and join the crowds, leaving his pedal cycle among lots of other bikes parked near the official car park in the grounds of the Hall. Then he would walk down a back lane into town, a short distance but out of sight of everyone, commit his crime and use the same back lane to regain his bike, always out of sight from the town centre. And then, having altered his appearance slightly by changing some clothing, he would make his way home via the back lanes between Brantsford and Ashfordly. But on 25 May, we were waiting for him or his brother, or both.

CHAPTER 7

One of the sad outcomes of most crimes is that the perpetrators seldom know or try to understand the consequences of their actions or the traumatic effect upon their victims. What is a mere theft in the mind of the criminal, perhaps done on the spur of the moment to earn a spot of extra cash, can, in the victim's eyes, be a most harrowing tragedy which might affect them for the rest of their lives. It is not only the deprivation of their treasured belongings, it is often something very emotional which follows.

Here is just one example. An elderly lady of my acquaintance suffered a raid on her house and lots of her possessions were stolen. She lived alone but was away on holiday with relatives at the time. The house was somewhat isolated and the burglar was able to work undisturbed at the rear of the premises until he had literally emptied the house of its valuables. He must have spent a lot of time at the house and he must have had a vehicle to carry away the goods but no one saw or heard anything. It was a very cleverly planned attack.

The difficulty from my point of view was that the lady, who was in her late eighties, had no real idea what had been stolen nor indeed did we know the precise date of the raid. She found the disturbance when she returned after a month with her cousin in the south of England which meant the thief had probably enjoyed a long start over us. He had forced a lock on a flimsy rear door and had closed it upon leaving, thus making the house appear normal to anyone passing by; a close look at that rear door, however, would have alerted a keen observer.

By the time we learned of the burglary from the distraught householder, the property would probably have been disposed of and it would be impossible for us to trace it back to the criminal, even if we had recovered any of it.

Another problem from the investigative aspect was that everything which had been stolen had been kept in boxes or wrapping paper; the thief had emptied cupboards, shelves and drawers in his deliberate attempt to remove as many items as possible, taking the boxes and wrapping paper in which they had been stored. It seemed to me he had not opened any of those packages to check the contents—he'd simply taken the lot and so I had to ask the unfortunate victim how she had come to have such a large hoard of wrapped or boxed goods in her house. She told me lots of the stolen items were silver, china or glass, but there was a wide variety of objects.

'They were my wedding presents,' she told me through tears. 'My husband was an army officer and at our wedding reception he was called away; there was some kind of emergency. We hadn't even time to cut the cake or unwrap the presents. I don't know what the emergency was but he left immediately so I decided I would keep all the presents in their wrappings until he returned. He never returned, Mr Rhea, he was killed on duty, in France. The First World War, you know.'

I calculated that those wedding presents had been in that house, in their boxes and wrappings, for more than fifty years. It was the saddest of stories and I wondered if the thief realized just how much unhappiness he had caused. Even if some of those presents were of modest monetary worth, they had a massive sentimental value.

As I tried in vain to elicit useful descriptions from her, I was concerned that the thief had struck so effectively during her absence. It was odd he had taken the gifts which were still wrapped or in their boxes—so had he known what he was stealing? Was the thief someone known to the lady? A relation perhaps? Someone who knew what she was keeping and that she would be away from home at that particular time? Maybe I was wrong to suspect the thief had been someone known to her, or very close to her from a family relationship point of view, and the culprit was never traced. In spite of our efforts in circulating a somewhat incomplete list of stolen property to antique dealers, second-hand shops and salerooms throughout the country, and making extensive enquiries in the locality, not a single item came to light. Even if a piece had turned up somewhere, I doubt if we could have proved it had been stolen from that particular house. Had we shown a recovered item to the old lady, it is doubtful whether she would have been able to positively identify it, particularly if it had never been out of its box. That thief was on to a winner, and I think he knew it.

If he had been a mere opportunist burglar, though, would he have taken all those treasures if he had known the sad story behind them? It is a question none of us can answer—most of us cannot and do not think or behave as thieves, and most criminals have no feelings for others and no conscience.

Having said that, there is some honour among thieves because some thieves have, over the years, displayed surprising acts of humanity, not only to those of like mentality but also to members of the general public.

I've known a burglar ring the police, anonymously, because he discovered evidence of child neglect and abuse in a house he raided; I've known another ring the police upon finding a dog starving to death in a locked house, and I've known several cases where thieves and burglars have returned stolen goods when the press have publicized the tear-jerking stories which resulted from their crimes.

Then there was the case of Jamie Appleton's bike.

Jamie was a bright twelve year old, tall for his age and the only child of Lucy Appleton whose husband had died tragically in a car accident when Jamie was only three. Lucy worked as a dinner lady in the school, the hours permitting her to rear her son even if the pay was very modest. But by being prudent and sensible, she earned enough for herself and Jamie, and she kept a very neat and tidy cottage which was rented at a low rate from Ashfordly Estate. She managed to give Jamie a few shillings pocket money each month, out of which she had taught him to save for the things he really wanted. And the thing he wanted more than anything else in life was a gents' bicycle with racing handlebars and ten-speed derailleur gears. Because Lucy's income was merely sufficient to maintain their quiet way of life without luxuries, however, the idea of Jamie buying an expensive racing bike was out of the question—unless he saved up for it. And that would take a long, long time.

To give Jamie due praise, he was not daunted by the prospect and over the years had assiduously put a shilling away each week towards his bicycle. He'd worked out that a shilling a week was fifty-two shillings (£2 12s. 0d.) per year, more than £5 in two years.

Some weeks he might save more than a shilling and by the time I first got to know him, Jamie had £17 17s. 0d. saved—that was when he was twelve. Not all of it had come from popping shillings into a piggy bank, however. He'd received useful sums of extra money for each birthday or for Christmas and realized he could earn even more by doing odd jobs like delivering newspapers, walking dogs, helping with haytime, harvest and potato picking, doing simple gardening jobs, even washing cars and going shopping for housebound people.

The snag was that new racing bikes cost an awful lot of money; he found one in a catalogue which cost more than £140 but it was somewhat special because it was the special lightweight kind used by riders in the Tour de France. His sights were more in the £25–£30 range, by no means enough for a brand-new machine. It was when he was about twelve and a half years old, that his mother spotted an advert in the *Ashfordly Gazette*. A man in Galtreford was advertising for sale a gents' racing cycle with 10-speed derailleur gears and a racing saddle, all in perfect condition and he was asking £22 for it. She showed the advert to Jamie who suddenly felt he must have this bike, even if it was second-hand; he had realized that the more he managed to save, the more expensive new bikes were becoming. Prices were rising all the time. He never seemed to have enough to buy a smart bike and so he knew he must act immediately—even if he had only seventeen guineas saved.

'The man might come down to twenty pounds,' said his mother.

'I've still not got enough!' he wailed.

'I've been putting a bit by as well,' she smiled. 'For your thirteenth birthday, when you become a teenager. If you like, we can go and see the bike, but it might have to be an early birthday present.'

Lucy Appleton was the first to admit she knew very little about ordinary bikes and even less about racing machines and so, because she'd discovered I had competed in road races in my teens and knew a bit about racing bikes, she asked if I would examine it. The owner's name was Jim Ashton and he worked in a solicitor's office in York but lived in Galtreford. And so it was that we all turned up to view the cycle at his home, by appointment. He was in his mid-fifties, I estimated, a tall, erect, slim and very smart man with neat grey hair and a pleasing manner. He wasted no time on pleasantries but led his party of visitors straight into a spacious outbuilding beside his house, and revealed the bike, shining and beautiful in its pale-blue trim. It was a Viking make, I noted, well-known in the world of mass-start cycle road racing.

'There it is,' he said, and I detected a slight hint of sadness in his voice. 'Have a good look at it, Jamie, and take it out for a spin if you like. I want to be sure the bike is suitable for you. You're a tall lad, I see, and it is a full-size machine. Lightweight alloy handlebars, lightweight frame, derailleur gears, ten speed, racing saddle, high pressure tyres with twenty-seven inch wheels though, they're bigger than those on normal bikes; it's a racing size. And the high pressure tyres need a special pump, there's one with the bike; rat-trap pedals with toe-clips, you'll see. Quick-release wheels, for changing tyres during a race . . . this one's got mudguards too, you'll note, but in some races, of course, they are removed. They can be detached very easily . . .'

After providing details of the cycle and allowing Jamie to handle it, twirl the pedals and spin the rear wheel off the ground, Mr Ashton persuaded him to wheel it outside into the daylight, then told him to lift it up by the crossbar with just one hand, just to see how truly lightweight it really was. He then invited Jamie to test the saddle for correct height and adjust it if necessary, then take the bike for a quick ride along the lane. Mr Ashton was most considerate in the way he dealt with the youngster, making sure the saddle was correctly adjusted even for Jamie's short trip and then showing him how to flip the pedals on starting to ride so he could push his toes securely into the clips. Within a few minutes, and after circling Mr Ashton's yard a few times, Jamie indicated he'd like to take the bike for a short ride along the lane and Mr Ashton smiled his consent.

'He's a natural,' he said to Lucy, as Jamie disappeared out of the gate. 'Good strong legs, fine sense of balance, knows how to use his ankles and toes on the pedals, you should encourage him to make full use of his skills.'

'It's a nice bike,' she smiled. 'I know he'll want to buy it. What do you think about it, Nick?'

While Mr Ashton had been highlighting the bike's qualities, I had given it a thorough visual check, and then I had wheeled it myself, noting there was no play in the bearing of the handlebars, the pedals were firm in the bottom bracket with no sign of worn ball bearings, either in the pedals or the bracket, and the wheel bearings were sound too. The gears worked well; in fact, its condition was as good as that of a new bike although I could see it was a few years old.

I thought it was a very good bicycle in tip-top condition and excellent value for the asking price.

'It's in superb condition.' I had no qualms about expressing that opinion. 'It seems hardly to have been used and it's been well kept, anyone can see that. I think it would be a very good buy for Jamie.'

'I want it to go to a good home,' stressed Ashton. 'I would never sell it to anyone I thought would not care for it.'

'You've had it for some time?' I asked, thinking that Jim Ashton did not look like a cyclist.

'It was my son's,' and that note of sadness returned. 'We bought it for his sixteenth birthday but, well, he died soon afterwards in a traffic accident. Not when he was riding his bike, I might add. We kept it as a kind of memento, I suppose. I've maintained it and ridden it myself, not a lot, just enough to keep things working efficiently, but I've decided it needs to be used much more regularly. Jamie wouldn't have wanted it to waste away . . .'

'Jamie?' I had to ask.

'Yes, I'm Jim, he was Jamie. Odd, isn't it? Your son's also called Jamie.'

'I'm not his father; he's lost his own dad,' I said. 'Lucy is his mum, though. I'm just here to examine the bike for her. I used to be a very keen cyclist.'

'Well, that's amazing. Here am I without my Jamie, and here's this Jamie without a dad . . . I think this is some kind of omen. I wouldn't want it to go to just anyone, you know, and if this Jamie wants my Jamie's bike, it would make me very happy. If he buys it, perhaps he'll come up here from time to time, to visit me and to show me how he's looking after it?'

Lucy smiled but wanted to discuss the price while Jamie was testing-riding the bike. 'I know he would, once he knows the story . . . now, er, Mr Ashton. The advertisement said twenty-two pounds.'

'To be honest, money is not my chief concern, Mrs Appleton. Of much more importance to me, and to my wife, is that Jamie's bike goes to a good home, to someone who will cherish it. I think it is good value, very good value at that price, but I am not going to haggle . . . make me a sensible offer.'

'Jamie's been saving for years,' she smiled. 'All his birthday money, newspaper round earnings, potato picking and so on. He's got seventeen guineas, all of his own, money he's raised by his own efforts over a long time and I know he wants to pay for it himself. Out of his very own earnings. I have a little saved too, for we do want to pay a fair price, Mr Ashton.'

'It's easily worth the asking amount,' I told her.

'Look, if Jamie likes the bike, he can have it for what he has saved,' said Ashton. 'On one condition.'

'Which is?' asked Lucy.

'That he treasures it, looks after it and, as I said earlier, brings it here for me to look at once every so often.'

'I'll make sure he does all that,' she assured him.

Jamie bought the bike and promised all the things that Mr Ashton had wanted.

I was sure I detected a tear or two in Ashton's eyes as Jamie mounted his new bike and began his ride home with evident pride; we thanked him profusely. Mrs Ashton appeared at that stage and she was equally sad to part with her son's precious bicycle although she was delighted to learn that another Jamie now owned it. Even before he rode it away, I gave Jamie some advice about security of the precious machine, such as making a note of its serial number or even popping into the hollow handlebars or down tube, a piece of paper bearing his name and address. He assured me he would take the greatest of care with the bike and soon we were following Jamie home in my car. He rode well; boy and bicycle seemed as one as he sped through the lanes showing a remarkable talent for fast and safe riding.

In the months that followed, I saw Jamie riding the bike around the village and along our quiet lanes; the bike was always shining and clean, always kept in the peak of condition and I heard that he'd joined the Ashfordly Wheelers, a thriving cycling club whose members enjoyed outings and rallies in the region. I remember thinking that Jamie would soon find himself drawn to cycle racing—he possessed the easy grace and strength required to excel in that toughest of sports and those talents would increase as he matured into his late teens; I began to watch his career with interest. And he cycled out to visit Jim Ashton and his wife from time to time; through the sale, the Ashtons had acquired a new son.

Then tragedy. Lucy Appleton turned up at my house at 8.30 one Saturday morning; she was clearly distressed and was crying.

'Nick,' she sniffed. 'Someone's stolen Jamie's bike . . .'

I hurried straight around to her house. Jamie was waiting, in tears, and together we went to the shed in which he'd kept his precious machine. It was a stone outbuilding in the lane behind the house and it had a stout wooden door with a hasp, but hanging from the hasp was the remains of a small padlock. Someone had cut through the lock's shank with what must have been bolt cutters and the bike had vanished. I learned that Jamie had locked it away the previous evening around 8 p.m. and had found it missing this Saturday morning, just before his mother had come to my office.

Realizing how sad this was, and how upset both Jamie and his mother were, I had to adopt an official approach because it was imperative for all concerned that a description of the bike was circulated as rapidly as possible. I had to bear in mind the culprit might have a start of several hours, that he might have sold the bike immediately, that it might have been repainted or even dismantled, and that, whatever its current appearance, it might be a considerable distance from Aidensfield by this time. If there was to be any chance at all of recovering this bike, I had to act swiftly even if it meant temporarily ignoring the personal trauma of the situation.

There were two bonuses for me, however; the first was that Jamie had recorded the cycle's serial number which was stamped in the frame under the bottom bracket. Although some thieves might resort to filing away the whole or part of such a number, few had time to do so if they wanted a rapid disposal of their ill-gotten goods and in any case, such an act was an indication of malpractice. Anyone buying the bike legitimately should be warned off by this action.

The second thing in my favour was that Jamie had written his name and address on a piece of stiff paper and folded it into a tube which he had pushed into the hollow of his handlebars, near the left side hand-grip. The new tape which he'd used to bind the hand section of the handlebars had effectively concealed and safeguarded the paper. If we found the bike, the chances were that the piece of paper would not have been found and removed; it could seal the fate of the thief.

After duly commiserating with Jamie and his mum, I rushed off to Ashfordly Police Station to set in operation the procedures to deal with the theft. The crime was circulated to all local police stations by radio, with a complete description of the missing cycle, and I knew it would reach all patrolling constables within the hour. I made sure details were despatched to Force Headquarters for incorporation in the monthly Stolen Cycles Supplement which was handed to cycle shops, garages, dealers and even cycling clubs. In those well-established ways, news of Jamie's loss entered our records of current crimes.

In my heart of hearts, however, I doubted whether it would be recovered. The fact it had been stolen by breaking into a building with a set of bolt cutters indicated a knowledge of its whereabouts and a determination to steal that particular racing cycle. This was not the usual case of spotting a bike in the street and hopping aboard for a free ride home from the pub, and then abandoning this form of cheap transport. In such cases, these bikes were often found by the police or reported by members of the public, taken to the police station and stored, but seldom claimed.

York Police Station, even today, is renowned for being home to hundreds of unclaimed cycles, most of which have probably been stolen, or 'borrowed' without permission within the city, and yet not reported missing. In due course, all unclaimed cycles are sold by auction with the money going into county funds, although every month or so, members of the public are invited to search the collection for their own missing machines. A very small percentage are actually claimed. I didn't think Jamie's bike fitted the category of a casually stolen cycle although I would make sure he visited police stations in the locality to search their stores of unclaimed bikes. As I did my best that morning to pay special attention to Jamie's loss while wondering when Jim Ashton would learn of the loss and how he would react, it was Alf Ventress who put forward one suggestion.

'Your new duties take you into Eltering from time to time, don't they?' he said later that Saturday as he wallowed within a cloud of cigarette smoke.

'They do, Alf,' I agreed. 'Is there something you want?'

'Not me, no, but it's just that Bike Mad Barney Barrett lives there. He might be worth a visit,' and Alf then began to search among his card index of known local thieves. 'If I were you, I'd get there as soon as you can.'

'Bike Mad Barney Barrett?' I smiled. 'I've never heard of him!'

'He was active before you were posted here,' smiled Alf, pulling out a filing card. 'His address is on this card along with details of some of his old crimes. Barney will be in his late sixties now, long retired from crime of course. I don't think he will have nicked that lad's bike, but he might have heard something on the grapevine. Even though Barney's retired, he still gets thieves approaching him when they want to dispose of stolen bikes, he knew the receiver's trade inside out, probably still does. He used to nick a bike, have it stripped to pieces within the hour and another bike rebuilt from its parts, and parts from others, so it was unrecognizable. Then he'd sell it locally. He got caught sometimes, but not every time, not by a long way. Try him, Nick. Bike mad he was, thought of nothing else, stole nothing else, but he's quite a pleasant old character now. Take it from me, if some local villain has stolen that bike, Barney will be able to find out for you, there's nothing in the stolen bike world that gets past him. He loves bars of milk chocolate, I remember. And he's got a soft spot for kids too. Go and see him, Nick, ask him if he can help.'

I lost no time driving to Eltering and went straight to Barney Barrett's address. It was nearly twelve noon that same Saturday when I found him in his workshop. I tapped on the door and walked in to find him making an ornamental garden gate from pieces of scrap iron. Even though I do not claim to know much about such work, I thought this was an excellent piece of craftsmanship and complimented him upon it.

'Ah, a new officer!' he smiled cheekily. 'Heard of my reputation, eh? But I'm not active now, young man, no stolen bikes for me, this is all legit. I buy the scrap, make the gates and sell 'em, a nice occupation for me, and a chance to earn a legal bob or two while filling all this leisure time. So what brings you here? We've not met, have we?'

'Nick Rhea,' I introduced myself. 'From Aidensfield, I'm the village bobby there, this is not my usual patch, but I'm acting sergeant for Brantsford and Ashfordly. As Eltering is my sub-divisional headquarters, I visit it now and again.'

'So you've come about a missing bike I bet? My reputation lives on!'

'Alf Ventress suggested I call, I need help.'

'Help? The constabulary asking me for help? Now there's a fine how-do-you-do!' and he grinned wickedly. 'Times have changed, eh? Give Alf my regards, he's a wise old owl, you know. So what's this help you want, Acting Sergeant Rhea?'

I told him about Jamie's stolen bike and provided a complete description which I'd recorded on a piece of paper; I handed this to Barney.

'I never did that, you know, I never broke into places to nick bikes. The ones I took were all just left lying around the town, standing against railings or left at the railway station, forgotten or abandoned I should think in most cases, and I never knowingly took a kid's bike. If a kid had a full-size bike though, and left it carelessly in town, then yes, I might have nicked it, but I'd never wittingly take a child's bike . . . but you say this is a full-size racing bike?'

I emphasized the characteristics of Jamie's bike, then told him about Jim Ashton's role in selling it to young Jamie.

'Is that the Jim Ashton who works in a solicitor's office? Lost his own lad in a traffic accident a few years ago?' he asked.

'That's him, a real nice man. He wanted Jamie Appleton to have the bike; he wanted it to go to a good home and now this has happened. I don't know whether Mr Ashton knows about the theft yet, it only happened this morning, but he'll be devastated when he finds out.'

'He once did me a favour, that Mr Ashton, when I wanted a solicitor and couldn't really afford one. I won't tell you what it was, just to say I owe him one, Mr Rhea. Right, leave this with me. Give me your telephone number and I'll see what I can do. No promises, mind. And no questions asked if I get it back, right? That's what I want. No questions asked.'

I wasn't quite sure of the implications behind that final condition, for police officers could never normally operate on the 'no questions' principle but I heard myself agreeing to his terms—for the sake of young Jamie. I admired some of his other work which was stacked around his workshop, then left to drive back to Ashfordly. I told Alf what had transpired and he smiled.

'Barney will do his best,' was all he said.

When I returned to Aidensfield, I called on Lucy and Jamie to explain the procedures we had initiated in an attempt to find his bike, but I did not mention the possible role of Barney Barrett. I did not want to build up Jamie's hopes unduly and then I went home. On Sunday, I carried out a further search of any likely dumping place for the bike, feeling that it was highly unlikely this splendid machine would have been dumped, but one had to carry out all such basic procedures. I found no sign of the bike that Sunday.

On the Monday, I was scheduled for 'cover' duties, that meaning I was on duty all day without specific hours. In the absence of any other supervisory officer, I had to cover the entire section from 6 a.m. one day until 6 a.m. the following morning, not necessarily working in the office all the time but certainly on call during those hours. At 8.39 that Monday, therefore, I was just about to depart for Ashfordly when my phone rang. 'Aidensfield Police,' I responded as normal. 'Acting Sergeant Rhea.'

'Barney Barrett, Mr Rhea,' said the caller. 'That bike you were asking about. Get yourself up to Highfield Barn, just above Highfield Farm outside Slemmington. It's there, waiting for the lad. Untouched, good as when it was taken. I've dealt with the thief.'

'Dealt with him? How?'

'That's my business.'

'But Barney, who was it? I mean, what did you do? Where did you find it?'

'No questions, Mr Rhea, remember? Just go and collect the bike,' and he replaced the telephone.

I stared at my handset for a few long moments wondering how the bike had come to be there, wondering also what Barney had done to achieve this, if in fact it was due to his efforts, and puzzling how he had contacted the thief with such speedy results. But, as he had said, I must not ask any questions. I rang Ashfordly police office where Alf was on duty and told him I was taking my van out to Highfield Barn, a derelict building on a very isolated moorland road above Slemmington.

It took me some forty-five minutes, but as I walked into the deserted old ruin, there was Jamie's bike in the same state as I'd seen it when he'd bought it. Taking the wheels off by using the quick-release hubs, I packed it gently in the rear of the van using some old sacking which was always there for a variety of reasons, and turned for home. I called at the police station in Ashfordly *en route* and informed Alf of our success, whereupon he would circulate a message to all stations saying, 'As a result of information received, the stolen cycle has been recovered undamaged'. Then I drove to Aidensfield and deposited the bike in my own police office for a while because Lucy would be at work and Jamie at school. I would restore it to Jamie later in the day. Later, when I returned home for my tea, I rang Lucy.

'Ah, it's Nick Rhea, Lucy, is Jamie there?'

'Yes, shall I call him to the phone?'

'No, just tell him there's something else I need to know about his bike. Can you get him to call in?'

'Yes, of course, when?'

'Now?' I suggested.

'Yes, yes, of course, he's so miserable . . . I do hope they find it . . .'

And so Jamie came to the police house wondering what else he had to tell me and I had great delight in surprising him with his recovered bike. He wept with joy, brushing with his hands its paintwork, its handlebars, its saddle and its mudguards and I suggested he might like to buy a very stout lock for his shed. He asked me how we had found it and I told him it was all due to a gentleman in Eltering.

Jamie, ever thoughtful, said he would like to thank him, so I gave him Barney's address and said, 'All you have to do, Jamie, when you're on a long ride, is pop in and see Barney, but make sure you have a few bars of milk chocolate to give him. He loves them!'

'Thanks, Mr Rhea.' He tried to shrug off his tears of joy. 'I must be going.'

'Look after it,' I said.

'I will,' he promised. And so he did—and a few years later, he rode it in his first race, an event for juniors. He came third but I knew that one day he would win.

* * *

A similar case occurred when confidence tricksters paid a visit to 83-year old Mrs Phoebe Sellers who lived in a council bungalow on the edge of Elsinby. It was a classic example of a confidence trick. The two men knocked on her door one lunchtime when she was struggling to make herself a meal, and announced they had come from 'the council'. One of them waved some kind of document in front of her as a form of identification and then they said they had come to check the house because there was some kind of scheme planned for insulating the walls and roof. Did she mind if they looked around and took a few measurements?

One of them remained in the kitchen with her, chatting amiably about the scheme and how it would benefit her while the other ostensibly explored the house, tapping on walls, climbing into the loft, taking measurements with a long tape measure and making a great show of doing something important. After a few minutes, the wandering man returned, said he'd got what he wanted and they left.

'I thought they left in a bit of a hurry,' she told me afterwards. 'But I never thought they'd been into my bedroom . . .'

They were crooks of the most despicable kind, preying on defenceless people and in this case while one had kept Mrs Sellers occupied, chatting happily about the huge benefits that would soon be hers, the other had been scouring the house for her savings. And he had found it. Like so many people of her age and background, she kept a tin box under her bed, and into it she placed the money left over from her weekly housekeeping, most of it being tiny amounts of savings from her meagre pension. All sorts of other small personal treasures were kept in that box too, such as a pair of silver earrings given to her by her late husband on their silver wedding anniversary, and a small photograph of her own parents.

That was a Victorian image in an oval brooch which was the only picture of her parents she had. Everything had been stolen, the box included. I had no idea how they had smuggled it out of the house because she could not recall them having a hold-all or a similar bag. Her money box was quite large, one of those black metal ones with a carrying handle and red and gold lines around the lid. She thought it was about eight inches long by five inches wide and two inches deep, large enough to contain a considerable amount of cash, but she could not give me a precise figure for its contents. She thought it was nearly £900, her life savings in fact; she kept all her money there because she did not trust banks.

Sadly, she could not provide a very accurate description of the men, other than to say they were young, quite tall, dressed rather scruffily and one had long fair hair. By the time I was told of this raid and obtained these details, almost half an hour had passed and I knew the chances of catching them were remote—they would empty the box at the first opportunity, throw it away and keep the cash. And her precious photograph would also be discarded. Even if we did find the men, we might never recover her belongings.

In this case, though, I had a wonderful piece of good fortune. Phoebe's neighbour, a retired policeman called Reg Harvey, had chanced to be in his garden shed when the men had arrived and, knowing Phoebe rarely had visitors, had instinctively noted the registration number and description of the car without them realizing he was observing them. He'd also seen the men hurry from the house, get into their car and drive off at speed towards Craydale. His suspicions aroused, he had gone straight round to Phoebe's house to find out what had happened, and then called Ashfordly Police. It took them time to contact me because I was on a foot patrol without radio contact. Precious minutes had been lost. I interviewed Phoebe about it and her distress was visible and when I called on Reg he confirmed she was extremely distressed about the loss of her family treasures—they meant more to her than the money. I lost no time circulating a description of the car so that all patrolling police officers, including those in cars, would know of the crime and, as the car number was one of the series of North Riding numbers, I could ring and obtain the name of the registered owner—and have a police officer awaiting his return home.

The registered owner was a man called Alan Simpkins who lived on a housing estate on the outskirts of Scarborough. I rang the CID in Scarborough, told them the story and Detective Sergeant Oakland assured me he would despatch one of his officers to await the return of Simpkins. He told me that Simpkins and a companion called Joseph Henry Brown had long been suspected of this kind of confidence trick but they'd never been able to convict them of any crimes. That was largely due to the elderly victims being unable to provide clear descriptions of the suspects and, of course, the fact the villains discarded everything except the stolen cash. In this case, however, we had a good reliable witness in that former policeman; later, I would re-visit Reg Harvey to see if he could tell me anything more. I was aware, as Oakland had warned me, that Simpkins or his pal would have thrown away the money box and contents soon after driving away— but would have kept the cash.

If they had thrown away this money box, it might be their undoing if I could find it—surely, it would bear the fingerprints of one of them? That should be enough to secure a conviction. As I knew, the road between Elsinby and Craydale was a long winding lane stretching to almost two and a half miles. Reg Harvey said they had driven off in that direction which meant they had probably cast the unwanted box out of their car and over the hedge somewhere along that road. Could I find it and so provide irrefutable evidence of their guilt? Knowing the road very well, and thinking it would surely be the passenger not the driver who threw away the box, I decided to check the route without delay.

I would park my police car at given points and search the verges and hedges along the route—it might be a long job taking a few days, or I might strike lucky and find the box very quickly. It took me a couple of hours. I felt the thieves would not have discarded the box close to the village outskirts, indeed just over those hedges were gardens and allotments where a box would be easily spotted, so I began about half a mile on the Craydale side of Elsinby. Parking my police van, I began to check every yard of the nearside verge and then I found it. It was on the banks of a stream where the road crossed a small bridge. I guessed they'd hoped the box would drop in the water and float downstream or even be submerged, but it had landed among some briars and so I recovered it, paying due attention to the likelihood of it bearing the fingerprints of one or both of those men. The lid opened easily without handling anything but the handle and I saw it contained the family photographs although the silver earrings were missing—and, of course, there was no money left. But it would be preserved for our Scenes of Crime Department. I decided to tell Phoebe that good news.

When I arrived, Reg was with her, trying to offer some sympathy and help in the aftermath of her plight but my good news was just the tonic she needed. I explained there might be a delay until the Scenes of Crime Department had checked the box and its contents for fingerprints but I assured her she would have her precious photographs restored to her. As I explained I could not offer the same reassurance about the earrings nor the money, Reg interrupted.

'Nick,' he smiled. 'If you can catch those villains with the money, we might prove where it's come from. Phoebe has a note of all the serial numbers on the notes!'

'You have?' I asked with some surprise.

'Yes, Mr Rhea, numbers fascinate me. I once found my birth date—day, month and year—in the serial number on a ten-shilling note, so I saved it and then, when I began to keep all my savings like I did, in that box, I recorded each note's number in a notebook . . .'

She explained that when she tucked away her unspent cash, she liked to know how much was left if she had to dip into the tin for extra spending money—and the finest way was to record each note's serial number. If she was unsure whether or not she had dipped into the tin, she could check the numbers of the uppermost notes against her notebook, and so determine whether or not she had spent one. She kept all the notes in separate piles according to their denomination—ten-shilling notes, pound notes, five-pound notes and even one ten-pound note, all with elastic bands fastened around them.

'I must tell Scarborough CID about this!' I said. 'They're waiting for these rogues to go home . . . we must catch them with the loot.'

I rang Detective Sergeant Oakland from Phoebe's telephone so that the maximum speed was achieved and I told him we had a complete list of all the serial numbers of the stolen notes and he expressed his utter delight.

'Can you get them over to me somehow?' he asked. 'Photocopy them if possible . . . if we nail Simpkins and Brown, this'll be just the ammunition we need.'

And so it transpired. Simpkins and Brown were intercepted on their way home and, apart from spending just one pound note on some petrol, they were caught with all the stolen money in their possession. They had divided the spoils before getting home and so each was caught red-handed in possession of stolen notes. The earrings were found too, Brown's fingerprints were found on the money box and Phoebe got everything back.

When I learned the date of the court case, I made sure the local press knew about these villains—the story of their disregard for the plight of their elderly victims would alert others to them and their cruel tactics.

Both men received a sentence of twelve months' imprisonment.

CHAPTER 8

If criminals rarely understand or foresee the distressing consequences of their selfish behaviour, then neither do many
other members of the human race. Police forces throughout
this country, and indeed across the world, can relate examples
of thoughtlessness or sheer stupidity which have produced
dire or fatal results—ill-prepared people getting lost among
the mountains and requiring the services of mountain rescue
teams, sometimes with fatal consequences to a team member;
people going out to sea in flimsy boats and needing help from
the lifeboat; people getting lost on the moors with volunteers
going out seeking them in atrocious conditions . . . the list is
practically endless but the point is that so much distress can
be prevented by just a modicum of forethought and sensible
planning. It was once said that the emergency services mop
up after the unwanted residue of society and there are times
when police officers and others in public service wonder
about the intelligence of so-called adults.

In some cases, lots of unnecessary work is caused, and
precious time lost, by a simple lack of communication
between the relevant parties and such an example occurred in
Aidensfield when a group of elderly people decided to organize a bus trip to a pantomime in Scarborough. It was *Jack and*

the Beanstalk with some famous names among the cast, and it promised to lighten the dark evenings of that January for the audience in general, and for the Aidensfield bus trip in particular. The organizer was a retired secretary called Jenny May Binks who had been prompted to arrange the trip when so many old folks said they'd like to see the show but had no means of travelling to Scarborough and back, especially at that time of night.

At rather short notice, Jenny May asked Arnold Merryweather if he could provide the necessary coach for forty people but when he checked his previous bookings, he found he could convey the Aidensfield trip to Scarborough in time for the start of the show, but could not bring them back. He was committed to another function later that evening but, being Arnold, he said he would ensure that another coach operator brought them home. This was done very frequently, he explained; coach operators were a friendly bunch of rivals who could be guaranteed to help one another in crises of this kind. Arnold said the second coach would turn up outside the theatre at the end of the show and it would halt on the way home for a late-night drink as she had desired. There was nothing for Jenny May to worry about. Arnold would pay the other operator out of his earnings. All the desired requirements would be accommodated. It was a standard form of sub-contract, he assured Jenny May.

And so it was one early Wednesday evening, Jenny May's pantomime-goers assembled at the war memorial in Aidensfield. It was six o'clock on a chilly dark night but Arnold would deliver them directly outside the theatre doors well before 7.30 so they would not be hanging around in the cold night air. They could go straight in to their pre-booked seats and would be collected immediately outside the door when the performance finished about quarter to ten. Arnold told them that the substitute bus would be one from Barlow's Coaches of Eltering, easily identified because all Barlow's buses were light blue with white roofs and dark-blue lettering spelling Barlow's Coaches across the rear.

After the show, the Aidensfield party, a mixture of men and women of all ages, albeit mainly of the senior citizen age group, emerged from the theatre in a jolly frame of mind, all looking forward to a brief stop on the return journey when they could buy a drink or two in a pub, or even have a nice cup of tea or coffee. Coach drivers on such occasions always chose the venue for these stops and because tonight's driver wasn't Arnold or one of his employees, they looked forward to his choice of pub or café. It would be a nice change from the pub where Arnold usually took them. Variety was the spice of life, as someone said. And so they all boarded the waiting coach, chattering happily after a most entertaining and enjoyable evening. The driver asked, 'Everyone here?' whereupon Jenny May said, 'Yes, everyone's on board,' and the bus drew away from the theatre on its homebound journey.

I might never have known about this outing had it not been for Oscar Blaketon who rang me at eleven that evening to say there was a crowd of strangers hanging around the war memorial, making a lot of noise by their incessant chattering and their attempts to keep warm. He had spotted them as he'd been locking up his pub at closing time.

'So who are they?' I asked.

'Search me, Nick, they've not been in my pub, I can tell you that. They're all standing there now, about forty of them I'd say, men and women, chattering and trying to keep warm. They're not locals.'

'I'll go and have a look,' I promised him. 'But are you shut? I know you can't serve alcohol at this hour of the night but if they need somewhere warm to wait, perhaps with a coffee or something, can you cope? There's nowhere else open.'

'If it'll help, yes,' he agreed. 'It does look as if they are waiting to be collected by someone.'

And so I replaced the handset and set off to see what was going on. I was in uniform and so, as I approached the group, my oncoming presence was observed and they all fell silent as they watched me, with, I felt, no little degree of concern.

'Hello,' I spoke to them all at the same time for I could not discern anyone who appeared to be in charge. 'Can I help you?'

No one responded. They looked at me in total silence, in much the same way as a herd of cows looks at a stranger at their field gate. Very quickly, I began to suspect these people needed more help than I could give. 'Are you waiting for someone?' was my next ploy.

'The bus,' said a little man with a twitch to his face. 'We got off and it's gone.'

'Where's it gone?' I asked.

'Don't know,' said the man.

'Where were you going on the bus?' I asked.

'Home,' said the little man.

'And where is home?' was my next question.

'Er . . . I don't know . . . where is home?' and the little man turned to another standing at his side.

'Pineview,' responded the other man. 'Pineview Nursing Home.'

'Ah!' I knew the home. It was near Eltering and catered for people with mental difficulties. I tried again. 'So you have been on a bus. Where did you go?'

'To see Jack and his beanstalk,' said the first man. 'It was real funny . . .'

'So a bus took you to see *Jack and the Beanstalk*. Where was that?' I asked.

They all looked at each other, shaking their heads and muttering to one another so I said, 'Why did your bus leave you all here?'

'He said it was where we got off.'

'Do you know where you are now?' I put to the group.

Again, there was lots of shaking of heads and muttering, but no one mentioned Aidensfield and so I said, 'Look, I will try to find your bus. I think we should all go and find some-where warmer and perhaps a coffee or cup of tea . . .' and I led them like a crocodile of schoolchildren to Blaketon's pub.

His door was open and the bar fire was still burning; he had been watching my encounter from a distance and

146

said, 'You'd better fetch them in, Nick; they look frozen and frightened. I've got some tea and coffee brewing, and biscuits . . . so what are they doing here?'

'I'll tell you when I get them all settled, Sarge.' I still called him Sarge even though he had been retired for a long time. And so we settled them all on seats in the bar as Blaketon and Gina fussed over them with coffee, tea and biscuits.

'So what's going on?' Blaketon came to me again.

'They're from Pineview,' I said. 'So far as I can gather, they've been to see *Jack and the Beanstalk*, and I think they've got the wrong bus home.'

'A party went from here to see it tonight,' he said. 'Jenny May organized the outing; it's at Scarborough. So they've come here from Scarborough, you think, on the wrong bus?'

'Sarge—' a ghastly thought now struck me—'if these people have come here by mistake, where do you think the Aidensfield trip has got to? Have they come home?'

'I'll check,' he offered.

He rang Jenny May's home number and got her daughter who said her mother hadn't come home yet. She was later than expected, but it might have been something to do with getting another bus because Arnold couldn't bring them home. So Blaketon rang Arnold Merryweather.

'Oh aye, I fixed up the return trip with Barlow's,' said Arnold. 'I had summat else on, why? Haven't they come home yet?'

'No, but thanks, Arnold. We'll get this sorted out,' said Blaketon. 'Nick, I think this one's for you—you're the law. How about ringing Pineview to see if they know where their folks are?'

I found the telephone number in Blaketon's directory and rang the nursing home. A woman answered.

'My name is PC Rhea from Aidensfield Police,' I introduced myself, in the hope my call would sound very official. 'I have a party of people here with me and I think they're from your nursing home. They've been to a pantomime at Scarborough . . .'

'Oh, no, Constable, you're mistaken,' said the woman. 'Ours have all returned, they're in the lounge now having their cocoa.'

'So who have I got here? There is a party of people, around forty of them, who have been dropped off a bus in the middle of our village having been to the pantomime at Scarborough tonight, and they say they're from Pineview.'

'Well, I don't know what to say. I'm on night relief; I've just come on duty and usually deal with patients when they're all in bed . . . I don't really know them all that well but I'm sure we've none missing. I would have known if any of our people were missing.'

'I'm not suggesting you've any missing,' I said, 'I'm suggesting you might have an extra complement of residents. Is there someone senior I can talk to?'

'Well, we're not supposed to disturb Matron unless it's an emergency and . . .'

'Tell Matron this is an emergency. Tell her it is the police calling and I must speak to her. Can you put this call through to her?'

'Yes but—'

'Then do it,' I snapped.

A few moments later a sharp voice responded. 'Yes?'

'Matron?' I asked.

'It is, and who is that?'

'PC Rhea from Aidensfield,' I introduced myself again. 'I believe a party of your residents went to the pantomime at Scarborough this evening.'

'They did. I trust they have not been causing trouble, they were sensible people, Constable, or so I thought, otherwise we would not allow them to attend a public event of that kind. So, tell me, what is the problem?'

'Have they returned?'

'I went off duty at ten, Constable, when the night detail came on duty, but if they had not come back on time, I would have been told.'

'Can you check?' I put to her. 'I want you to check because I have forty people here in my village, all claiming to come from your establishment. I suspect they caught the wrong bus after the pantomime, and were dropped off in Aidensfield in error. And a busload went from Aidensfield to the same pantomime and they have not come home yet. Which means—'

'Oh my God! You don't mean we've got your villagers here?' she cried. 'Well, I mean, if there has been some terrible mistake . . . oh dear, I mean, Constable, we do get a lot of our residents claiming they should never be in here, and with different shifts on duty, often with temporary staff, I suppose mistakes could be made . . . Look, I must go and check. Where can I contact you?'

I gave her Blaketon's telephone number and said I would remain until I had heard from her.

'It can happen,' laughed Blaketon. 'Two buses from the same company waiting outside the theatre. The Aidensfield lot climb aboard one that's going to the nursing home and off they go; who's going to believe them when they say they're not from the home?'

'Surely, someone should realize they're not residents!' I laughed.

'In time, yes, but straight away? Imagine this: they get dropped off at the door of that home, probably thinking it's a nice hotel or something. I know the place, it is a handsome building you know, a former manor house, most impressive entrance. So the bus leaves and they go inside where cocoa's waiting in the lounge . . . it'll take a few minutes for them to realize they're in the wrong place, then who's going to believe them when they say so? Who, among fairly low-ranking nightshift attendants, is going to let them out, Nick? They'd never do that . . . and who's going to believe they don't live there?'

'So the other bus, the one that's supposed to bring them home to Aidensfield, is then boarded by the people from the nursing home and when the driver gets here, he just says "Right, folks, that's it, you're home" and they all get off to find themselves marooned in the middle of our village. Arnold Merryweather's going to have to answer a few questions about all this!'

When the matron rang back she was desperately sorry for the mix-up and said it must have been due to a lack of communication between the respective bus companies or even the bus drivers. She told us that the Aidensfield bus load had climbed off the bus and walked into the home, to be guided by a night-time nurse into the lounge where cocoa and biscuits were waiting. They thought it was a routine stop at a nice hotel—in fact, the outer aspect of the home had the appearance of a nice hotel even if the interior was not quite up to that standard. But they had settled down to the cocoa and biscuits. When Jenny May had said to a hovering member of staff, a new girl, that it was time they were getting home, no one would believe them. The girl thought they had come home safely and the doors were securely locked because the staff had heard that kind of thing so often before . . .

'I think this is a job for Arnold,' said Blaketon. 'He can take these people back to Pineview and fetch our lot back here. Shall I ring him or will you?'

* * *

Another event which caused undue complications began with the most simple of activities—a man taking a dog for a walk. The gentleman in question, a visitor to Elsinby, was taking the black and white cur-type dog along the road to Aidensfield. It was a nice spring morning, just approaching ten o'clock, and there had been some overnight rain. The roads were just a little damp and slightly greasy, but in spite of that, there had been no reported incidents or accidents, and for man and dog, everything was straightforward and simple.

The dog was on a lead and being walked along the wide grass verge which allowed him to sniff and explore a galaxy of interesting sections of the hedgerow. The lead was long enough to permit him a good degree of freedom to explore, but short enough to prevent him from wandering on to the carriageway. But the happy dog startled a rabbit which had been hiding in the hedge bottom and it bolted across the verge and on to the road. The dog, sensing some exciting sport, lunged violently against the lead and the sudden unexpectedly sharp tug caused the man to release his grip. In an instant, the dog was free to chase the galloping rabbit which he did with some gusto. And the man, reacting instinctively, lunged after the trailing lead.

Unfortunately, an articulated tanker was coming along the road at that very moment and the driver, seeing first the dog leap into the highway and then its owner make his lunge for the lead, braked as hard and as quickly as he possibly could. In spite of his efforts, he lost control and the front nearside wing of the lorry hit the man and sent him spinning into a gatepost as the dog (and the rabbit) escaped. His fierce braking manoeuvre caused the rear section of the tanker to jackknife, which in turn had further affected his control of the cab unit. As the cab struck the unfortunate dog walker, so the trailer section swung around to its offside causing the entire tanker to slide out of control, slew across the road and finally overturn.

The front part, including the cab, came to rest near the gateposts while the rear section slid along to finish partially above a ditch at the far side of the road. The entire road was blocked because the tanker lay on its side, completely filling both carriageways. The man had been knocked unconscious by either the lorry or his collision with the gatepost and he was lying on the verge. Rather miraculously, the lorry driver was unhurt apart from some bruising and it was he who later provided an account of the incident, but as he extricated himself from the cab to survey the damage, he realized the tanker section of his vehicle had cracked. A very ghastly-looking fluid was seeping out and dripping into the gutter which was full of fast flowing water.

That gutter drained the adjoining fields; excess water entered the gutter which in turn flowed into Elsinby Beck and thence into the River Derwent to make its somewhat convoluted way through miles of countryside and lots of villages before entering the North Sea.

Not only that, before coming to rest, the free-ranging tail-end of the tanker had collided with the fence on the verge above the gutter, and an entire section of the fence had collapsed. The field contained a herd of cows which, as herds of cows do, came to inspect the trouble, found the hole and, without wasting a moment, decided to explore the area beyond its home field, i.e. the road. Then a motorist, a representative specializing in supplying veterinary practices, came upon the scene and went to a nearby farm to summon help. Acting swiftly and positively he found the farmer's wife and with her help, rang the doctor, the ambulance, and the police, saying the road was blocked and heavy lifting gear would be required.

His call went to Eltering Police Station, whereupon the duty constable rang me, urging me to make a rapid assessment of the situation and inform him in case emergency action was required. The inspector had been in the office at the time and instructed him to warn me that we might need to call chemical experts and the fire brigade; he suggested the fire brigade may know how to cope with the worrying spillage but that was by no means certain. I was urged to supply the situation report with the minimum of delay. Fortunately, I was on duty and I was already in the office attached to my police house and about to embark upon my peaceful and quiet daily routine.

The fact I was in such a state of readiness meant I was aboard my van within seconds and heading for the mayhem, wondering what dramas awaited. As I drove the short distance to the scene, I recalled the words of one of my earlier sergeants. 'Never rush to the scene, son,' he advised me. 'Take your time; don't arrive breathless; don't arrive in a state of panic. If the policeman panics, it makes everyone else nervous. So take your time and on the way, try to work out what you will do when you arrive—but first, protect human life. That's essential, your first consideration. Top priority. It can include anything from administering first aid, to stopping oncoming traffic to reduce the dangers . . . so there you are, protect life. That's your priority, and whatever you do, do it with a display of confidence.'

His words went around and around in my head as I motored towards the scene. I was approaching from Aidensfield of course, and when I was about half a mile away I was confronted by the sight of a herd of about fifty Friesian cows being driven towards me. At first, I thought this was quite normal—it could be a farmer returning his herd to a field after milking, or it might be one removing his herd from one field to another, but as I halted to allow the herd to pass, I realized there was no man with them. They were being driven along by a black and white dog who seemed to know what it was doing and, as the cows slowed down at my approach, the dog barked and ran behind them to encourage them to keep moving forward. I halted and within seconds, the herd was past and heading for Aidensfield. At this stage, of course, I had no idea these animals had escaped from their field, nor did I appreciate the significance of the black and white cur-like dog. And so I let the cows pass, thinking that some farmer had placed complete trust in his dog, as indeed many did in moorland farms, and resumed my journey.

Moments later, I arrived at the scene to find several cars parked with their drivers standing beside them viewing the carnage from a distance, and so I moved closer with my van, my purpose being to have the official radio as near as possible to the scene. My first impressions were of a huge vehicle lying on its side completely across both carriageways, a man lying in a farm gateway, several people, men and women, moving around among the mayhem and a man in overalls trying to gain some kind of control over it all. My arrival, or to be more honest, the sight of a police officer in uniform, was clearly a relief to everyone and so, with my sergeant's words ringing in my mind, I walked into the centre of things. I realized that the man in overalls was the tanker driver; a logo on his breast pocket matched one on the overturned vehicle, but as he hurried towards me so did a tall, thin man in a smart suit.

'PC Rhea,' I introduced myself and knew I must establish my authority. 'The local policeman. Let's start with that injured man . . .'

'I've called the ambulance and doctor,' said the man in the suit. 'I haven't touched him, he's alive but unconscious, I thought it best not to move him in case he's got a spinal injury or damage to his head; he got a nasty knock by the look of it.'

I hurried across to the still form in the gateway; a middle-aged man wearing a woollen jumper and corduroy trousers was lying on his back and I could see a trickle of blood oozing from one ear, the classic indication of a fractured base of the skull. I touched the man's face, his skin was hot and his face rather flushed. His breathing was noisy too. These were further signs of a fractured base of the skull, or a compressed fracture of the skull.

'We shouldn't touch him,' I said. 'It looks like a compressed fracture of the skull; the ambulance has been called, has it?'

'Yes, I called them. They said they'd be here in ten minutes, that means any time now,' said the man in the suit. It might sound callous to leave the casualty lying there but I knew that any movement by inexperienced people could prove fatal.

'Have you moved him?' I asked the man in the suit and the lorry driver.

Both assured me they had not, both adding they knew better than attempt any first aid on such a casualty. I made a note of the name of the man in the suit—Paul Milner, the representative for a veterinary medicine manufacturer—and discovered he lived in Craydale; he had not witnessed the accident but had been first on the scene and had responded with sense and speed.

I asked if he knew the name of the casualty, but he did not. Although he lived fairly locally, he'd not encountered him and had no idea who he was or where he was from. I told him that if he wished to do so, he could leave now, all the emergency services were *en route* and there was nothing he could do here, unless he was prepared to help me in one small way.

He said he was more than happy to do so, and I pointed out the line of parked vehicles on the Elsinby side of the blockage; clearly, traffic from the Elsinby direction was building up and I had 'DIVERSION' and 'ROAD BLOCKED' signs in the rear of my van. I asked if he would place them on the Elsinby side of the accident to divert traffic via Ploatby and Thackerston. He said he would be more than pleased and off he went to collect a couple of signs.

'Thanks.' I was most grateful to him. 'If I don't see you again, I'll call on you later to obtain the necessary witness statement for my accident report. I'll see to things at the Aidensfield side of the pile-up, if I've time!'

'Just one other thing before I go,' he said. 'I noticed the fence at the other side of the road has been smashed down by the tanker. I come through here most days on my way to Ashfordly and there's usually cows in that field . . . I did pop down to the farm again, where I used the phone, to mention it but there's no one in. Odd, when you think about this mess on their doorstep.'

'Cows?' I said. 'What kind of cows?'

'Friesians,' he said.

'Oh crumbs. I drove through a herd of them on my way here, being driven the other way, towards Aidensfield. By a dog. Fifty or so.'

'It sounds like them,' he said.

'Not a black and white cur?' The lorry driver now said his piece.

'Yes, it looked in control. I assumed it was a herd being returned to their field somewhere along this road!' I had to tell them.

155

'It's this chap's dog,' said the driver. 'He had it on a lead when I first saw him, and it got away, chased a rabbit across the road and he dived after it, which is why I braked like I did . . . the dog got away.'

'Does the farmer know his cows have been rustled by a dog?' I asked.

'No,' said Mr Milner. 'There's nobody in. I spoke to his wife first time and now she's vanished. You'd think they would be out here, finding out what's happened.'

'This isn't the farmer; I know him.' I pointed to the unconscious casualty as a thought struck me. 'Maybe it's one of his workers?'

'No, the farmer's called Ryan, I know him well enough too. I'm sure it's not his labourer either. Unless he's a new chap. Look, I'll go back to the farmhouse to see if I can find Mr Ryan, then I'll position your road signs. You've enough to do here.'

'Thanks.' As he departed about this new mission, I turned my attention to the lorry driver but at that moment, Doctor Archie McGee arrived.

'Morning, Nick,' he sounded cheerful. 'A nice start to your day, eh? So what have we here?'

I indicated the casualty who was still unconscious in the gateway and provided as much information as I could, then McGee asked if he had been moved in any way; when I confirmed he had not, he nodded his head and said, 'Good, the less movement the better. Ambulance on its way, is it?'

'It should be here any minute now,' I told him, knowing it would have to fight its way through the string of cars which was gathering on the Aidensfield side of the incident, not to mention negotiating a herd of promenading cows which, I guessed, were still being driven towards Aidensfield by the casualty's dog. But at this point, there was no one I could despatch in pursuit of the dog or cows—I just hoped the dog was as clever as we hoped, and that it would spot an enclosure of some kind and drive the cows into it.

'Who is he?' asked the doctor, as he crouched to carry out his initial examination.

'I don't know,' I admitted. 'I haven't seen him before and I haven't searched his clothing yet.'

'I need to know, or the hospital will need to know so we can tell his relatives. But let me examine him first, then I'll worry about who he is.'

And as the doctor began his task, I turned again to the lorry driver. 'Right,' I said. 'First things first. Are you injured in any way? We've a doctor here; I think you should let him examine you.'

'Nothing more than a few bumps and bruises, I braced myself when I felt the truck going. I'm more worried about that stuff dripping out of the tanker,' he said, pointing to the rear of the vehicle. 'It's going into that gutter and is being carried off by the water. God knows where it will finish up.'

This reminded me that I might have a possible major incident on my hands; I had been concentrating on the state of the casualties and those missing cows to the extent I had momentarily forgotten that something nasty was dripping into the water courses.

I hurried across and saw the steady drip of something which was oozing from a crack beneath the tanker and falling into the ditch water before flowing away but in the meantime, turning the water green. I could not smell anything and it seemed to be a modest amount of pollutant. 'What is it?' I asked the driver.

'Search me!' he shrugged. 'I'm just the driver.'

'You mean you don't know what you're carrying?' This occurred in the days before compulsory labelling of vehicles which carried toxic or dangerous substances.

'No, I'm just a relief driver, the real one went sick this morning and I was called in last minute.'

'Where have you come from?'

'Stockton-on-Tees,' he said. 'National Chemicals. We're sub-contractors. We supply the tractor units, then we go to the depot, hitch up to the tanker trailer detailed for us and take it to wherever we're told. I'm taking this one to Hull.'

'I need to contact your depot,' I said. 'My office will do that; I'll radio them. We need to find out if this stuff's dangerous.'

'You'd think they'd tell me if it was!' he snapped. 'But nobody said I had to be extra careful or not sniff it or get it on my hands or whatever.'

'Right, I need to see your papers right now, and either your place of origin or destination,' I said. 'And I need to know before we try to move this thing.'

As he went off to search the debris in his overturned cab, the ambulance arrived and I accompanied the two attendants, one of whom was the driver, to the side of Dr McGee. He stood up now.

'Fractured base of the skull, I'd say,' he warned them. 'He's unconscious and might remain in that condition for some time. Be careful with him.'

'Who is he?' asked the ambulance driver.

'I've no idea. I've searched his clothing, but there's nothing. Just a door key and a handkerchief. When he gets his clothes off, there might a tattoo, or he might have a bracelet or necklet or something which will lead us to his relations, but so far as I can see, he's not carrying any form of identification. No wallet, diary, nothing. So off you go, gently on to the stretcher with him and I'll ring the hospital to say you're on your way.'

As the ambulancemen went about their expert handling of the casualty, Dr McGee said, 'If the hospital can't find any identification on this chap, Nick, you might have to use your network. I don't know him, he's not one of my patients, so I wonder if he's a holidaymaker in one of the local cottages? Funny he should be walking a cur along here though. It could be a pet I suppose. I'll be in touch; must be off now. I've a busy round of patients waiting for words of comfort.' And off he went, the lorry driver reiterating he did not wish to be examined. Dr McGee didn't argue—he had enough to do without unwanted extra work.

As the casualty was being gently carried to the ambulance on the stretcher, Mr Milner returned.

'I've found the farmer and his wife,' he said with evident relief. 'They were both in the buildings. They've got a cow calving and it's a difficult birth. He'll go and look for those cows. They are his dairy herd. I've told him he'll have to take a long way round until this lorry's moved, he can't get past it here. He did say one thing, Constable.'

'Which is?'

'That dog doesn't belong to him so he can't understand why it's decided to drive his cows away.'

'It belongs to the casualty, according to the driver. He saw the chap with it on a lead just before the accident. If we find it, we'll treat it as a stray, we can keep it at Ashfordly Police Station until it's claimed, or we can put it in a dogs' home.'

'Fair enough. I see our human casualty's been removed, so there's just the lorry now!' he smiled. 'I'll go and put these signs out, then I'll be on my way. The long way round!'

And at that stage, the lorry driver returned clutching several pieces of paper. He found the one which authorized his company to collect the tanker unit from the Skeller Depot in Stockton-on-Tees, and he also produced the sheet which gave him permission to hitch his cab unit to the tanker trailer. Then he said, 'Here you are, Constable, the address in Hull. I've got to deliver it there. Well, I had to, they might have to drain it all away to get this thing back on its wheels or tow it somewhere.'

The delivery address in Hull gave no indication of the type of premises to which the load was being transported. It could have been a building site, chemical manufacturer, paint manufacturer, pharmaceutical producer, food company, household polish-maker, mustard-making company, car-seat manufacturer, carpetmaker, plastics factory, shoemaker or anything else—even a butcher, baker or candlestick-maker. And none of the paperwork provided the name of the chemical on board. Fortunately, there was a telephone number as a contact point—'In case of difficulties and problems of delivery' as it stated. As I went to my van, I told the queue of waiting motorists that it would be some considerable time before the road was clear and advised them to turn around and find another route, asking them to look out for a herd of cows heading towards Aidensfield with a dog in charge. If the cows were noticed, I beseeched them, could they spare the time to ring Eltering Police to tell us where they were, adding that it was a request from me? I also asked one driver, whom I knew to be from the area, if he would position some 'ROAD CLOSED' signs on the exit from Aidensfield. He readily agreed and he helped himself to a couple from my van. And, I added, we would like to know the whereabouts of the dog too, if anyone spotted it.

As I was calling Eltering Police via my radio, the fire brigade vehicle, a small red van quickly followed by a break-down vehicle equipped with heavy lifting equipment arrived. Both drivers spotted me as I made my call; I acknowledged their arrival and said I would be with them in just a few moments. In the call to Eltering Police, I provided the contact number of the firm in Hull and asked PC John Rogers, the duty constable, to ring them, tell them about the accident and ask if they could identify the stuff in the tanker.

I explained that the fire brigade expert had just arrived, along with a heavy duty breakdown vehicle, that the unknown casualty had been removed to hospital, that something nasty was dripping into a small water course, and that a herd of Friesians had escaped and were intent on a walkabout. John Rogers said he would note everything I said and would endeavour to contact me—perhaps if I returned to my radio in, say, twenty minutes? I said I would do that.

As I was walking back to the stricken tanker, Don Ryan, the farmer, arrived. I'd met him previously when I'd been to his farm to check his stock registers and firearm certificate. He was in his early sixties, a dour Yorkshireman with a pleasing sense of humour and when he saw the sights near his farm entrance, he said, 'I don't know what you've got out here, Mr

Rhea, but we've just got a new calf. Sorry I didn't get out here sooner, but when a cow's in need of maternity care, you've got to stay with her.'

'No problem, Don—except all your other cows have gone walkabout, through that hole in the fence.'

'Aye, that chap Milner said so. So where are they? Any idea? I thought I'd better check with you before I set off looking for 'em.'

'Last seen heading for Aidensfield along this road, with a dog in charge,' I told him. 'That was shortly after ten o'clock.'

'They'll not be far, Mr Rhea, cows aren't ones for going on long walks. So whose is the dog?'

'I think it belongs to the casualty, he's been taken to York Hospital. He was seen walking it along this verge.'

'Well, I hope it doesn't drive 'em too far, Mr Rhea. I've got to get myself ahead of 'em and then drive 'em all t'way back here.'

'You can't get through this way, the lorry's blocking your gateway and the road so it'll mean a long trip round by Ploatby and Thackerston if you're going to get ahead of them,' I told him.

'No it won't,' he grinned. 'I'll get my tractor and go through my fields. I can be out on that Aidensfield road in less than two hundred yards. Right, I'm off.'

'If that dog's still with them,' I laughed, 'will you fetch it back with you? We can keep it at the police station until the owner decides what we should do with it.'

'If it'll come with me, I'll fetch it along, but if it doesn't want to come, then I shan't go chasing it and trying to persuade it.' He was adamant about that.

'Fair enough, it's not your problem, Don.'

'Is there owt else I can do for you before I go?'

'It's just a case of dealing with the tanker now,' I told him. 'The heavy lifting truck's arrived, and the fire brigade, so we'll cope, thanks.'

And as he turned away to leave us, I went back to the lorry driver who was in discussion with the fire brigade officer and two men with the heavy lifting vehicle. I explained I had asked my office to contact staff at the lorry's destination in an effort to identify the load and so we spent some time discussing how to lift the tanker back on to its wheels.

In fact, it did not seem unduly damaged and it might conceivably be driveable, although something would have to be done about the spilling load. It would require a relief tanker to take it away as we all knew it must not be driven along public roads with some unknown liquid dripping from its containers. As I awaited the passage of those twenty minutes before returning to my van, I measured the scene and made a rough, not-to-scale sketch of the lorry in relation to its position on the road. I would require these for my accident report when I submitted it, although the sketch would be drawn to scale before being finally sent in. And then I returned to my van.

True to his word, John Rogers returned my radio call and produced some reassuring news.

'The load is not dangerous, Nick. The only effect it will have will be to colour everything green. It's a concentrated vegetable dye used in the food industry. For colouring ice-cream, would you believe! Making it green; for that mint-flavoured stuff, but the dye's not minty. The flavour comes from something else. The tanker is in sections inside and only one section will be affected; the others won't drain into the damaged part so there's no need to empty the lot—that's if the heavy lifting gear can cope with the nearly full load. And by the way, we've had a call from ex-Sergeant Blaketon. He says there's a herd of Friesians on the village green at Aidensfield, helping themselves to the grass, leaving indented hoof prints all over the place and, worse still, dropping messy cow claps wherever they go!'

'All in a day's work,' I said. 'Right, thanks, John. We'll see what can be done here and I'll call again when the road's clear. The farmer's on his way to collect the cows. Did Blaketon say anything about a dog being with them?'

'He did. A black and white collie or cur. It's sitting on the green, watching the cows. He reckons it drove them there, and now it's keeping them there.'

'Sounds like a clever dog. Right, we can forget the cows so that matter's cleared up. The farmer might see to the dog too. Any news from the hospital?'

'No, the casualty has not regained consciousness and no one knows who he is. He's got no documents on him. Although he's suffered a nasty bash on the head, he's not considered to be on the danger list.'

The skills of the men with the heavy lifting gear managed to hoist the fallen tanker back on to its wheels and when it was upright, the green dye stopped flowing out. No one knew how much dye had entered the water course which was now coloured a vivid green, along with the rocks, earth and plants over which it flowed. It was now possible to tow away the tanker. The driver did not feel it could be driven even though it did not look too badly damaged; he was fearful that the steering mechanism or brakes might have been affected, or even the articulated section. A wise decision, we all thought.

Farmer Don was left with a fence to mend and a herd of cows to drive all the way back home, but, funnily enough, he was helped by the black and white dog which seemed to enjoy driving livestock from one place to another.

I went home to write my report and later that evening, I received a call from York Hospital.

'Dr McGee asked us to contact you if and when the Elsinby Road casualty regained consciousness, Mr Rhea,' said the ward sister. 'Well, he is now conscious and as comfortable as can be expected. He's off the danger list and we are very pleased with his progress. He will be examined in some detail by our specialists, but is not yet fit to be interviewed about the accident. Perhaps you would like to check with us in say, a couple of days?'

'Yes of course, but do you have his name and address? I need that for my report.'

'Yes, he is Mr James Edwin O'Malley; he comes from Leeds and he was staying in a holiday cottage in Elsinby.'

'Ah, right. And his relatives? Have they been informed?'

'He's a widower but has a son living in Cambridge, Mr Rhea. He has been informed and will travel to Leeds to stay in his father's home, pending a hospital visit to his father.'

'Thanks. And just one other thing, Sister, for my report. His dog. Did he say what he wants done with his dog?'

'He hasn't got a dog, Mr Rhea. He told me it was a stray he'd found. It was trailing a lead so he took the lead and was taking the dog back to the village when the accident happened. The dog is not his, Mr Rhea, he was adamant about it. He's never seen it before.'

'Well, whoever it belongs to it, it's certainly made its impact in this part of the world! But thanks.'

When I told Don Ryan the dog had no known owner, he said it was a good, well-trained farm dog, very capable at driving cattle and sheep and he offered to keep it until the real owner came along to claim it. Very oddly, no one did come to claim it. It was a most peculiar outcome because the dog was undoubtedly accustomed to working with livestock and had been very well trained. I wondered how its owner could have neglected to make a search for it. However, the dog stayed with Don and his wife, and he called it Green Lad, Greenie for short.

CHAPTER 9

One of the senior ladies of Aidensfield, senior in advanced age rather than social standing, was known to everyone as Aunty Phyllis. She lived in a neat stone-built bungalow not far from the pub, and when I arrived in the village she would have been around eighty years of age. It was a long time before I knew her surname—which happened to be Walsh—because everyone referred to her as Aunty Phyllis. The butcher delivered to Aunty Phyllis, the newspaper girl had Aunty Phyllis on her list, the milkman's records showed Aunty Phyllis and even the vicar referred to her by that name, with no reference to her surname.

Aunty Phyllis was the sort of person who was always around the village and who could be relied upon to help other people in all sorts of small ways. She'd even go shopping for the 'old folks'—many of whom were younger than she—pottering into the grocer's or butcher's to secure something for her friends' meals. She had been married but her husband had died when she was in her early sixties and he had left her a comfortable income with the nice bungalow, on top of which she had a small Civil Service pension of her own from having worked in the administration department of Ashfordly Head Post Office. There were no children of the marriage, but she did keep a few cats. Somewhat surprisingly, she had no nephews or nieces although she claimed some distant cousins. That meant she was no one's genuine aunty, but because she was a kindly, friendly soul who could be seen out and about at most times of the day, she appeared to be a universal aunt.

Everyone needs a kindly aunt and everyone in Aidensfield, young and old alike, had one in the form of Aunty Phyllis. She had done lots of baby-sitting in the past, I discovered, and would always look after a child or even several children if the parents asked her. As a consequence, lots of the parents referred to her as Aunty Phyllis when discussing her in front of the children and so the name had stuck; she would be Aunty Phyllis for ever and a day.

In appearance, she was a large lady, almost six feet tall and sturdily built with a mop of thick white hair and the round, ruddy face of a country dweller. She was always cheerful, always interested in other people and always eager for people to drop in to her cosy home for a chat and a cup of tea. Aunty Phyllis could be relied upon, at a moment's notice, to provide tea, a piece of cake or a biscuit or two, all flavoured with a friendly chat or some homely advice. She liked to keep abreast with any local news and, I am sure, she was also at the centre of the village information network, spreading news about the place—although she could keep a secret when necessary. In short, Aunty Phyllis was one of the characters of Aidensfield; the place would not be the same without her.

During the course of my constabulary duties, I would pop into her comfortable living-room on a regular basis, sometimes for nothing more than a chat and the inevitable cup of tea, but sometimes to test her extensive knowledge about local people and their foibles. I did not treat her as a police informer, however; I did not expect her to be a sneak and give away family secrets; instead, she was more like an open book of facts and information about the people and their village. She knew almost everything about the place, from snippets of local history to the somewhat complicated relationships of the older residents. If I wanted to know who was related to whom (and how), all I had to do was ask Aunty Phyllis.

For all her loveliness and charm, she had one irritating habit. She was always late for appointments or events of any kind. If there was a play, film show, whist drive or any other event in the village hall, she would always arrive five minutes after it had started. She attended the local Anglican church on Sundays, and always arrived five minutes after the service had begun. If someone wanted her to be a baby-sitter in their home, she would arrive late, and if anyone offered her a lift in their car to Ashfordly, she would never be ready on time. Those who knew her well were perfectly aware of this weakness, and if they wanted her to baby-sit, they would ask her to arrive a quarter of an hour before they really required her, and this seemed to work as she would arrive ten minutes before necessary.

The vicar had tried to delay the start of his services by five minutes in the hope her late arrival would not disturb members of the congregation, but when he tried that, she began to arrive five minutes after he had begun at his new time—ten minutes later than the real time. It was an exasperating trait, but most of the village realized nothing could be done to persuade Aunty Phyllis to change. Being late for things was part of her unchangeable character.

As she had grown older, however, she had developed another deep interest—like so many people of her generation, as her friends, neighbours and acquaintances began to die, popping off one by one, Phyllis decided she should attend every funeral. Lots of village people did this on a regular basis—I have referred to some in earlier volumes—and so Aunty Phyllis joined that army of regular funeral-goers who turned up in all sorts of distant places at chapels, churches and crematoria.

Having no car, she had to rely on public transport which meant she would often arrive in a village long before the official time of the funeral, but even if the bus or train was on time and got her there well before the formalities had started, Phyllis somehow contrived to be late arriving in church for the funeral service. No one was quite sure how she did it—she wasn't one for spending time in the pub to while away the time. Even if she was offered a lift to the church by friends, she would somehow vanish for a few minutes, probably enjoying a walk—and would then arrive after the service had started.

One of my courtesies, as the village constable, was to be present at any of the churches on my beat whenever a funeral was being held. I made a point of arriving in good time to keep the entrance clear of cars so that the cortège could park as near as possible to the lych gate or main entrance. This was not any sort of formal duty—if we rural constables were informed that a funeral was to take place in any of the villages upon our patch, we would do our best to attend in duty time so that we help things to run smoothly, particularly from a motor traffic point of view. It was very important that the funeral cortège should proceed with the necessary dignity.

Our services in this respect were appreciated and it was while performing such duties that I would often see Aunty Phyllis rushing towards the church, puffing and panting and holding on to her hat, as she tried to get seated before the service began. And invariably she failed.

Typical of her problem was the story related to me by one puzzled villager. He said, 'It was last Saturday, and she decided to attend awd Ben's funeral at Thackerston. It was due to start at half past two in t'afternoon and she got t'bus which got in at quarter to two. Three quarters of an hour before t'service. And yet she was late. T'vicar had got himself warmed up for action, he'd got awd Ben into t'church and was just getting into being sad and sorrowful and saying that bit about him being the resurrection and the life when t'door opened and in trotted Aunty Phyllis. She wasn't content wi' taking a back seat either, she had to tramp right down to t'front because there was no seats at t'back. T'vicar was on about standing at the latter day and I thought she'd never find a pew, but eventually she got sat down behind t'relations just as t'vicar got to that bit about having the ungodly in his sights. But I ask you, what is there to do in Thackerston for three quarters of an hour on a Saturday afternoon? Nowt. But she did it and whatever she did or wherever she went, it made her late for awd Ben's send-off.'

Bearing in mind that Aunty Phyllis was into her eighties, and that she had become renowned throughout the district for being late at funerals, it was inevitable that people said of her, 'That woman will be late for her own funeral!'

She died peacefully one Thursday morning in December. She had been trotting around the village as usual the previous day, calling on people, having cups of tea and completing her daily chores. Then she had gone home, made herself a meal and settled down for a quiet evening before the television, the pictures of which were then in glorious black and white. A neighbour who had a car always popped in on Thursday mornings to ask if Aunty Phyllis wanted anything from the Ashfordly shops and usually had a chat with her over a pot of tea before leaving, but on this occasion, Phyllis was sitting in her fireside chair. The fire was out, none of her cats was in the house and the back door was unlocked. She had died in her chair, peacefully and apparently without pain or distress, probably while watching television the previous evening. Her set was still switched on.

In spite of her age, the doctor could not certify the cause of her death for she was not a regular patient and so we had to treat the matter as a sudden and unexplained death, which meant informing the coroner and arranging a post-mortem examination. Those were my responsibilities and I had also to attend and witness the post-mortem, the outcome of which was that Aunty Phyllis had died from natural causes—coronary occlusion as the pathologist recorded. So the coroner ordered there should be no inquest; the funeral could then proceed.

It was to be held in the Anglican church in Aidensfield at 10.30 a.m. on the Saturday before Christmas. A handful of distant relatives had been traced, cousins about the same age as Phyllis, and they had arranged a buffet with ham in the pub following the interment. To bury someone 'wi' ham' was considered an accolade. Because everyone in Aidensfield knew and loved Aunty Phyllis, as well as many who lived further afield, a large funeral was anticipated with lots of mourners and many cars. As things transpired I was working that day. I had completed my stint as acting sergeant but was not performing my usual beat duties; I was undertaking one of my occasional spells as the GP car driver. That meant I patrolled the whole of the sub-division for eight hours on a wide-ranging basis and instead of using my Mini-van, I had a large black Ford estate car loaded with enough equipment for me to deal with almost any incident from a road traffic accident to rescuing a climber from a cliff face. I thought this vehicle, which polished into a wonderful deep black, was ideal for me to use during my attendance at Aunty Phyllis's funeral.

When I booked on duty at nine that morning, therefore, I radioed Eltering Sub-Divisional Office to warn them I would be officiating at a large funeral in Aidensfield where heavy traffic was expected. I told them it was scheduled to begin at 10.30 a.m. and I expected to be engaged at the church for at least an hour. No one suggested I should do otherwise; there were no other pressing needs in the area at that time.

Having booked on duty, therefore, my first job was to visit Bernie Scripps, the village undertaker, to settle a few details before the event, such as the direction from which the cortège would approach the church, how many parking spaces I should reserve directly outside the church and whether there were any mourners who needed special consideration such as invalids or very elderly people.

Bernie explained that Aunty Phyllis's body would be brought by hearse from the chapel of rest in Briggsby, a matter of some two and a half miles; it had rested there since the post-mortem while her relatives had used her cottage and cared for her cats. The hearse would halt outside Phyllis's former home in Aidensfield where the relatives would join it in a fleet of vehicles, departing from the house at 10.25 a.m., and the entire cortège would then proceed sedately to the church. Bearers had been hired for the occasion, the funeral tea arrangements were complete, and an organist chosen to play the hymns of her choice. Everything necessary had been done—all we had to do was get Aunty Phyllis to the church on time.

As happens on these occasions, most of the mourners were inside the church, thinking it necessary to arrive early to ensure a seat, but quite a number milled around outside, renewing old acquaintanceships or just chatting, and then at 10.25 a.m. one of the churchwardens appeared. He wanted everyone to go inside.

'Five minutes,' he called to them. 'The hearse will be at the house now . . . everyone inside, please. Thank you, come along . . . that's nice, keep it going like that . . .'

I remained outside to supervise the parking of the hearse and cars which formed the cortège, and the moment everyone was inside I saw a middle-aged man in a black suit running towards me with anxiety all over his face.

'Oh dear, I need help, Constable, please . . . this is dreadful . . .'

'What's happened?' I did not know the man but it was clear he intended coming to the funeral and that he was not a mere late arrival.

'The hearse has broken down,' he said. 'Mr Scripps has been on the phone. I'm Phyllis's cousin, by the way, staying at her house . . . he's asked me if I can find another vehicle, he can't fix his hearse; the big end's gone or something very serious. I've been to the garage but there's no one there, they're all here or busy with the arrangements, and I don't know the district or where to go for help. Is there anything you can do?'

'Where is the hearse now?' I asked.

'Just out of Briggsby.' He had something written on a piece of paper. 'Near Fir Tree Farm, Mr Scripps said. That's where he rang from. It's on the road down from the chapel of rest. And it's got Phyllis on board, along with some flowers.'

'I know it,' I said, my brain working rapidly to recall any other undertakers who operated in this area. There was one in Ashfordly, I knew, and the Co-op operated a funeral service in Eltering but it would take ages to contact them and I knew it was a busy time of year for funerals, too. The chances were that all local undertakers would be busy, this being a Saturday and a popular day for holding funerals. Then I had a brainwave. My police estate car! It was smart, it was black, it was highly polished and if I removed all my emergency equipment and put the back seats down there was ample room for a coffin in the rear.

'I'll take my car, the black estate over there,' I said. 'I'll go now . . . you go into the church, find a churchwarden and tell him what's happened. He'll get the organist to play a few extra hymns . . . Briggsby's only five minutes away . . . say quarter of an hour for me to get there and back with Aunty Phyllis on board.'

At first, he looked rather dejected and somewhat askance at my bold suggestion, but when he saw the highly polished estate car, which did not bear any police signs, he smiled his agreement. 'Phyllis would like this,' he told me. 'She had a wonderful sense of humour, you know.'

'Keep them all in church,' I said. 'The chances are no one will ever know about the switch of vehicles . . .'

'Right,' he said.

And so, after unloading all my equipment and storing it behind the wall of the churchyard, I raced away towards Briggsby, never thinking that this mission might not truly be within the exigences of police duty. A few minutes later I was pulling up behind the stricken hearse. It did not take long to remove the coffin and flowers from the hearse and arrange them carefully in the rear of the estate car, but the snag was there was no means of securing the coffin. Bernie said he would sit with it in the rear and hang on to it— he also said I should drive, because it was a police vehicle and he wasn't sure whether the official insurance covered it being driven by an undertaker on a funeral mission. And so, with Bernie's assistant aboard in the front passenger seat and Bernie hanging on to the coffin in the back of the vehicle, I drove as slowly as I dared and with as much decorum as I could muster. I arrived at Phyllis's house where her relatives emerged into a fleet of waiting vehicles; no one appeared to notice that her coffin was not in a hearse and I understand her cousin had not returned to the house to explain things. He'd remained at the church to contain everyone until the arrival of the coffin and the cortège.

At the church, all the relatives left their vehicles and took their reserved seats inside and then the coffin was ceremoniously carried in by the bearers and placed before the altar. As I moved my estate car away from the church entrance, its role as a hearse now over, the organ was playing and the vicar was about to begin the service. Having parked my car, I walked back to the church door and could hear the familiar words of 'I am the resurrection and the life' from within, and then I glanced at the clock on the tower. It was five minutes to eleven.

Aunty Phyllis was late for her own funeral.

* * *

Another memorable funeral occurred in very strange circumstances. One Monday morning in June, I received a telephone call from the superintendent's secretary when she asked me to attend a meeting in Eltering Police Station on Wednesday at 2.30 p.m. When I asked the purpose of the meeting in case I had to prepare for it in any way, she admitted she did not know why it was being held, or what was to be the topic. All she knew was that certain senior officers and other people would be attending—and I should present myself in uniform.

As a consequence of that call, I spent ages wondering what I had done wrong, whether I was being posted to another station, whether I was being drafted on to some special task force or specialist unit, or whether I had been promoted following my spell as an acting sergeant. I could think of no other reason for such a mysterious summons to a meeting at Sub-Divisional Headquarters and so I spent the rest of that day, and all day Tuesday, pondering its purpose. And worrying to some degree.

On the appointed day, therefore, I arrived at Eltering Police Station at quarter past two in my best uniform with my trousers pressed, my tunic brushed and my boots polished. When I explained my purpose for being there, the duty sergeant showed me into the small conference room which adjoined the court house. The court house adjoined this police station and meetings of all kinds took place in the useful spare room. When I entered, I saw a round table set out with half-a-dozen chairs, blotting pads, lined foolscap notepaper and pencils, with glasses and a carafe of water in the centre. Cups, saucers, a plate of digestive biscuits and a jug of milk were on a side table. This made the whole affair appear somewhat important—specially to a mere constable.

I was first to arrive, but within seconds, Superintendent Clifford from Divisional HQ followed me into the room, accompanied by Detective Chief Inspector Andrews, both of whom were in civilian clothes. I brought myself smartly to attention at this influx of high-ranking officers, but was told to relax, and then three other men arrived, all in civilian clothes, whom I did not recognize. There was a good deal of hand-shaking followed by introductions and I learned these fellows were Mr Ferris, Mr Lake and Mr Johnson, but I was not told where they had come from or what their role might be. Three police officers and three apparent civilians.

'PC Rhea,' said Superintendent Clifford. 'We are all here, so perhaps you could tell the duty sergeant that everyone has arrived and ask him to organize the tea? And once the tea has been served, tell him we do not want to be disturbed.'

'Very good sir,' I said, wondering if my role here was to be tea boy.

As I went out to deliver the message, the others selected their seats and made themselves comfortable. When I returned, I found myself sitting between Mr Ferris and Detective Chief Inspector Andrews. Ferris was in his early forties, I estimated, a smart man with long, clean, brown hair and dressed in a dark-grey suit, white shirt and blue tie. Well spoken, he made polite conversation, asking me about the town's history, its castle and marketplace, adding that he was very unfamiliar with the north of England. Then the tea arrived. It was brought in by a young woman, one of the civilian staff employed in the sub-divisional offices. At Clifford's insistence, she poured us a cupful each, placed the biscuits in the middle of the table and departed. As she left, I saw a notice had been placed on the outer panels of the door—it said, 'Conference in progress, do not disturb.'

Superintendent Clifford, as host to this gathering, opened the meeting with the words, 'I need not remind everyone present that this is a top-secret meeting, and nothing of our discussions must be repeated outside this room. PC Rhea, for your benefit, I will say that certain matters have previously been discussed. This is called Exercise Molerun. As the meeting progresses, you will come to appreciate that you are here at this late stage because you possess important local knowledge, the value of which will become evident as we proceed. Now, Mr Johnson?'

Johnson was a rather plump individual with a balding head, rimless spectacles and a round, happy-looking face; in his early fifties, I thought he looked like a bank manager, or senior clerk in a solicitor's office. He lifted his brief-case on to the table and from it produced some sets of photographs bound in green folders. They reminded me of the booklets of photographs taken by the police at a traffic accident or at the scene of a crime. Everyone received one and he handed a complete set to me. In black and white half-plate size, they depicted a rather untidy graveyard from different angles including some from the narrow lane which passed the main gate. There was a shot of one remote corner near a drystone wall with a substantial yew tree standing guard. I recognized the scenes—this was Shelvingby churchyard. Shelvingby was a remote and very tiny village on my beat. I turned over each of the photographs but there was no caption on any of them and nothing in the booklet to identify the location.

'You recognize this place?' Johnson asked me.

'It's Shelvingby churchyard,' I said.

'You know it well?' was his next question.

'Reasonably,' I nodded. 'It's on my beat. I'm a regular visitor to the village as part of my duties.'

'And it is remote from the village? In fact, remote from anywhere; it's even about a mile from the church.'

'Yes, it is. It's near the river. Actually, the river's more of a moorland stream and in the spring parts of the graveyard have bluebells and daffodils growing all over.'

'So it attracts visitors and sightseers?'

'Very few,' I assured him. 'There is no public footpath along the riverside and parking is difficult in the narrow lane, so any visitors tend to be long-distance hikers passing by. It doesn't attract crowds and busloads, if that's what you mean.'

'Good. So it is one of the quieter corners of these moors, you would say?'

'Yes, certainly. Very quiet indeed. The whole area is well off the tourist trail.'

'And how quiet is the churchyard, and the road which passes it, during, say, the hours between midnight and five in the morning?'

'Deadly quiet,' I said, before realizing the joke. They all laughed, and it helped to lighten the somewhat serious nature of these opening moments. 'Normally, the only people likely to pass at that time would be late-night hikers or someone from the village returning after a night out, perhaps a game-keeper or two, but I doubt if any of them would venture into the churchyard anyway. There's no reason for local people to go wandering around it at that time of night. And, I might add, some of them would never go anywhere near a graveyard at night!'

'But you are saying that some people might use that road during those hours?'

'Yes. I can't guarantee no one will come along; there's usually someone around at any hour of the night as any police officer will confirm,' and I began to puzzle over this oblique line of questioning. 'As I said, though, I doubt they'd have any reason for going into the churchyard, they'd merely be passing by.'

'So if we wanted to conduct an exercise in that church-yard, without anyone seeing us at work, we would have to close the road? And arrange a diversion? Then because people might be abroad during the night hours, perhaps we need other security personnel actually in the churchyard?'

'Yes, if you want to keep absolutely everyone away, that would be the safest method,' I agreed. 'Are we talking about an exhumation?'

Johnson smiled. 'No, PC Rhea, the other way round. A burial. We want to carry out a burial, a human body complete with coffin, and we want to do it in that graveyard. We've even identified the site—it's the corner you've already seen in those photographs, number five.'

'A burial? In the middle of the night?' I asked, turning to the photograph of what appeared to be an unused plot of ground near a yew tree.

'Yes,' said Johnson. 'We want it to be done without any-one knowing, and when it is finished, we shall want the turf replacing so that it looks just like it does now. Undisturbed. When we leave the scene, we want it to look as if no one's ever been there. You can see, therefore, how important it is for us to carry out the burial in complete secrecy.'

'Am I allowed to ask who is to be buried there?'

'You can ask, but I cannot tell you. It is legitimate, by the way, we're not getting rid of a murder victim or someone who's caught the plague.'

Superintendent Clifford then said, 'I can confirm this is a genuine burial, PC Rhea. We are not proposing to dispose of ill-gotten goods, murdered bodies, hidden treasure or anything like that, nothing unlawful. This is simply a burial which must remain secret for reasons I cannot divulge.'

'If it is that sensitive, I cannot understand why you need me,' I had to say.

Johnson came in again. 'You have just confirmed what we suspected, PC Rhea, that people might be abroad even at those odd hours.'

'I would have thought that wasn't in doubt,' I heard myself say.

'Precisely, which is why we want you to be present to deal with inquisitive local people during our operation. We believe a local constable known to them is the best person for doing that. You can reassure them. Strangers doing mysterious things at night in their graveyard would only increase their curiosity and might cause unforeseen problems. We shall require the road to be blocked and diversions established as we carry out our plan and it is felt that if any of the locals came along and were met by you, they would accept your assurance that it is only a traffic accident that has blocked the road . . . or something equally feasible.'

'Most of them know me, yes,' I agreed. 'And if they saw me there on duty, yes, I agree, they'd accept my word.'

'Good, that is most important. Now, let us proceed.'

'If you are going to use lights, or make any kind of noise,' I said without being asked, 'I should remind you that such activity is bound to attract attention in such a remote place. The entire patch of moorland is in pitch darkness at night; there are no street lights. A light showing anywhere will be noticed. In particular, any bright light showing from the graveyard is bound to attract attention and I'm not sure the traffic accident idea would be foolproof, as they might wonder if it's anyone they know,' I told them. 'Why can't we acknowledge the lights and other paraphernalia by saying it's a film being made? For television perhaps? If I tell them they can see it on their screens in, say, six months' time, they'll accept it. If we try to keep them at bay, you can guarantee someone will try to breach our defences.'

'You think so?'

'I do, and some of those gamekeepers, and local lads, are very adept at moving out of sight and without a sound at night. I'd have difficulty stopping them from snooping. We need to put their minds at rest.'

Lake, a fair-haired, youthful man said, 'I agree with the constable, George. We can go ahead in accordance with our preliminary plans and have the road blocked and diversions established, but the cover story could be that a film is being made. That would account for the vehicles and lights, as well as any inadvertent disturbance to the vegetation that we might leave behind. People will accept it; they'll come next day, or at the weekend to see where it was shot, but that's all. They're not going to dig up the grave or wonder what else was going on, and they're not going to worry about one of their friends being hurt in a traffic accident.'

'Right, that's it, a film it is. Thank you, PC Rhea, a neat solution.'

'Just one point,' I asked, wondering about the formalities of doing this in a real graveyard. 'Have the church authorities been informed?'

'You will find the local vicar is away at a conference this weekend, PC Rhea,' smiled Lake. 'Now he will be told that his churchyard is being used as the scene in a film; his bishop will tell him so. We have taken care of those formalities, and can now tie up any loose ends.'

And so, having established the ground rules, the team settled down to discussing the time-scale and actual feasibility of digging a grave and burying a body in absolute secrecy at the dead of night. I had to remain at the meeting so that I knew everything that was happening, not so that I could tell the world about it, but so that I knew what *not* to reveal. I was advised that Superintendent Clifford would speak to my supervisory officers about my duties when the time came, and was told that if I was asked anything about my role I must say it was a command and control exercise to test our responses in a major incident—and leave it at that.

And so it was a few days later that at eleven o'clock one moonless Sunday night in July, I drove out to Shelvingby in my police Mini-van, my duty sheet showing a normal night shift from 10 p.m. until 6 a.m.; the sergeant had been told I was engaged on Exercise Molerun for the entire night and so, armed with my sandwiches, flasks of soup and coffee, apples and bars of chocolate, I made my way through the rising narrow lanes into the remote moorland place. On board, I had 'ROAD CLOSED' and 'DIVERSION' signs, an effective barrier which could be erected across the lane by one person, several 'POLICE' signs, some amber flashing lights fitted with batteries, the sort used by road workers, and a pile of plastic cones. I also had a map of the area in my van. From discussions at that meeting in Eltering, I knew where to position my signs; the van itself would also be used to block one end of the lane, at the junction beyond the churchyard from my direction of approach, the barrier would be at the other, and both would be reinforced by signs and lights. Furthermore I would be patrolling the length of it to ensure no one breached the signs although I now had some concerns that if anyone really wanted to breach our modest security they could do so while I was engaged elsewhere along the lane.

Half a mile was a considerable distance to supervise alone. I was sure there would be no major problems, however, not in such a remote part of the moors so I was confident I could cope with my modest part in this odd event. When I arrived, three vehicles were already there, all with men inside them and one was a van bearing the legend 'Flame Films, Dean Street, Soho, London, W.1' and a telephone number. If anyone rang that number, they would receive an appropriate response. As I parked behind them, Mr Lake emerged, followed by another constable in uniform.

'Ah, PC Rhea. Good to have you here. You'll see we have come equipped to make our film, so the sooner you get the diversions set up, the sooner we can begin. This is PC Ray Clarke from the Ministry of Defence; we felt you could do with a helper to control that length of road as it's rather too long for a lone constable, but he will act under your orders and will refer any queries by local people to you.'

Ray was a stolid individual with a southern accent, somewhat rotund in appearance, with a black moustache but wearing a cap like mine rather than a helmet. He could pass for a member of the local force—after all, we did have some southerners in the North Riding Constabulary. And so with Ray's help, I cordoned off the entire road past the churchyard; it was exactly half a mile long and was hardly ever used, but the detour through Shelvingby village almost doubled the distance. On the map, the roads were very like an equilateral triangle with the church along the base line; should any traffic head this way at night most of it would have ordinarily used the other route anyway.

One advantage was that, being a Sunday night/Monday morning exercise, traffic should be at its minimum. Because the village was perched on a hilltop, however, I knew that any lights in the churchyard, or on the roads nearby might be spotted by the residents—and even if they were on the point of going to bed or even in bed, they would surely come down to see what was going on. I warned Ray to expect one or two people as things got underway.

As I erected my 'ROAD CLOSED' and 'DIVERSION' signs, with 'POLICE' notices to reinforce the message, a gang of men emerged from one car armed with spades and pick-axes and got to work in the isolated corner of the church-yard. Although their area of operation was well screened by yews they'd also brought a large dark-green tarpaulin which they suspended on poles to form a very effective, all-em-bracing curtain. Then, with rather low-powered battery-fed lights, they began to dig. I thought the ground would be soft there—it was not far from the banks of the beck and usually quite damp.

Whereas I had anticipated they would be working in the full glow of arc lights fuelled from car batteries, they used the more modest glow from their lights so their activities would hardly be seen from the village or any of the surrounding farms. And as they dug the grave, I could hear them at work and wondered if we should have had a film camera or two, and a clapper board to give realism to this scenario, but there was no one about. We were the only living things near that graveyard—at least, that's what I thought as I wandered up and down my half-mile of road, chatting to Ray when we met during perambulations.

Then after about an hour, Mr Johnson arrived.

'Any problems?' he asked.

'Nothing,' I told him. 'I've not seen any local people at all, not one car's come to our barriers.'

'Good. Well, I'll go and see how our grave-diggers are coming along,' and off he went.

Then I had my first problem, albeit a minor one. A car pulled up at the barrier on the higher part of the lane and a man climbed out. It was about midnight and I went to confront him.

'What's going on?' he blustered. 'I want to get to Ashfordly. Can't I come through?'

'Sorry, sir,' I said. 'The road's blocked; there's a diversion through the village, it only adds half a mile to your journey,' and I showed him the road to take—the only one in fact. If he lived nearby, he would know it anyway.

'Well, it wasn't blocked when I came along just before eleven, I'm a vet . . . I'd just got home and my slippers on when I got another bloody call-out . . .'

'Sorry, sir. As I said, the diversion's a very short one, an extra minute on your journey, that's all.'

'So what's going on?' he demanded.

'They're making a film,' I said, and shone my torch on to the van with its logo on the side.

'Making a bloody film? And I've been inconvenienced just for that . . . this is not on, Constable, definitely not on. I shall write to my MP about this . . . mark my words . . . a bloody film . . . can they do this? Stage road blocks just to make films?'

'There were notices in the local papers,'—a white lie—'giving advance notice of a road closure. It's all perfectly legal, otherwise I would not be here. Now, if you have been called out to an emergency, sir, might I suggest you don't delay? And when you return, you'll find diversions will still be in force until about six.'

'Well, I expect to finish well before six; maybe when the pressure's off, you'll let me in to see how they make films these days?'

'We'll see how things progress between now and then, sir.' I smiled my most gracious smile. 'I hope your call-out is warranted.'

'A sick cat would you believe!' and he raised his eyes to heaven, then roared off to complete his journey.

When he'd gone, I went to tell Ray what had transpired should he be on the receiving end of the fellow's return trip, and we settled down to a long wait as the digging continued behind the canvas screen. It seemed to take a long time, but I had no real idea how long it took to dig a full-size grave, although I wondered if the diggers were going deeper than normal or if they'd encountered tree roots from the yews which flourished here, or they might have met some rocky shelves deep underground which would frustrate their work. As they worked, one or two passers-by arrived at my barriers.

There was a motor cycle with a young man and girl aboard, a man walking his dog some time after midnight and a courting couple who parked their car within sight of our operation. They seemed to ignore us as they set about the business of consolidating their love for each other, and then a lone hiker came past. He tried to bypass our barriers because he thought the restrictions only applied to vehicles. Ray encountered him and, after some heated words, persuaded him to take the detour. But that was all; no one else came to test our resolve and I don't think anyone tried to sneak into the graveyard from the other side—the river was a most effective barrier.

It was about 2.45 when Johnson decided it was time for a refreshment break and although we all stood around eating our sandwiches and drinking our coffee, we remained constantly alert, watching the road and never referring to the task in hand. But, it seemed, the grave-digging had been completed, hence the meal break, and then came the next stage. The coffin, lodged in the rear of the van bearing the film company's logo, had to be removed and carried, as unobtrusively as possible, along the path through the churchyard and into the screened-off area for interment. I had to guard one end of the cordoned-off road while Ray guarded the other and once we assured everyone that no one was around, the task of removing the coffin began. I made sure the courting couple's car had left—which it had—and so the simple coffin was covered with a black sheet and then borne by six men along the narrow path and through the forest of existing tombstones to the hole. I lost sight of it and could only hear the thudding of the earth being thrown back into the hole and landing on top of the coffin.

I heard no evidence of any kind of formality or religious service, and the refilling of the grave, although taking a considerable time, was far swifter than the digging. There was some surplus earth but this was placed carefully in sacks and carried to the rear of the 'film' van for disposal elsewhere. It was almost 5.30 before the screen was removed. Now, of course, the sun had risen and it was daylight; this essentially rural area was coming to life. Farmers would be on the move, early morning shift-workers heading to their places of employment, night shift-workers heading home and rural workers starting their day. There were cows to be milked, poultry to be fed and sheep to be checked and counted in their moorland paradise. Out here, life started very early.

Once the green tarpaulin had been taken down, Johnson said, 'Thanks PC Rhea, it's all gone very well. You can dismantle your barriers now.'

While the other anonymous men were completing their tasks, Ray helped me to remove my barriers, cones and signs and return them to my van; then within a surprisingly short space of time the place was back to normal. In the strengthening daylight, Johnson invited me to take a look at their handiwork and it was amazing. Each piece of turf had been replaced in exactly the same place it had previously occupied, all the surplus earth had been taken away and it would take some very close scrutiny to see that this patch of ground had been disturbed in such a massive way. There were a few particles of earth among the grass, but they would soon be absorbed by nature and in any case their presence would never hint at what had transpired during the night.

'That's it, PC Rhea,' said Johnson. 'Exercise Molerun has been successfully completed. Not a word to anyone, not for the next thirty years that is. By then, of course, all this will have been forgotten. So, thanks for your part in all this, you can go home now and so can we.'

And that was it. We all went home and I never knew who had been buried there, although about that time there was an article in a national newspaper to say that a top security official from the Kremlin had died in London after defecting to Britain and bringing with him a mass of secret information. The article said that, at his own request and due to fears of reprisals against his mortal remains he had been buried at a secret location. Whether he was buried at Shelvingby is something I shall never know, but stories of the mystery night-time film-making persisted for years afterwards.

And finally, as a matter of record now that the thirty years have passed. I can relate this story. Except, of course, that the secret grave is not really in Shelvingby. It is in another graveyard somewhere else deep within the wilderness which forms the higher reaches of the North York Moors.

THE END

ALSO BY NICHOLAS RHEA

Thank you for reading this book.

If you enjoyed it please leave feedback on Amazon or Goodreads, and if there is anything we missed or you have a question about, then please get in touch. We appreciate you choosing our book.

Founded in 2014 in Shoreditch, London, we at Joffe Books pride ourselves on our history of innovative publishing. We were thrilled to be shortlisted for Independent Publisher of the Year at the British Book Awards.

www.joffebooks.com

We're very grateful to eagle-eyed readers who take the time to contact us. Please send any errors you find to corrections@joffebooks.com. We'll get them fixed ASAP.

Printed in Great Britain
by Amazon

67043368R00113